Samantha gave Jarrett a cool smile. "Well, it was nice to see you again, Mr. Corliss, but I have to get back to my office."

She turned away, looking for the nearest exit, anxious to put distance between her and this too compelling man. He stepped close and stopped her, encircling her wrist lightly with calloused fingers.

"Not so fast. We're just getting warmed up here."

"The inning is over, Mr. Corliss. It's time for you to go back to the bench."

"Come on, Sammy, I haven't even had a chance to throw one yet. Have dinner with me tonight."

The question surprised her. The impulse to say yes surprised her even more. "Strike one, Mr. Corliss."

"Didn't I just put one right over the plate?"

"Sorry, no. That one was wild."

"Tomorrow night, then."

"No. Thank you, Mr. Corliss, but no."

She tugged away from him, but he let her get only half-free. He ran a finger down her cheek and over her chin. The touch was so electric that Samantha's hand tightened around his. All her good intentions vanished.

Dear Reader,

Having my very first book published by Harlequin American Romance has been a thrilling adventure! Thanks for choosing to read it; I'm glad you decided to join me.

The inspiration for this book came while watching a Little League game one warm spring day. Some of those nine-year-olds played so hard and so seriously. I wondered what happened to those boys as they grew up. Who would they become as young men? Would they still dream of hitting a home run or making a double play? And what would they risk to hold on to that dream? Their love for the game was so intense, what could possibly get in its way? And what about all those little girls who had dreams of their own? I had to know the answers to my questions, and *Man of the Year* began to unfold, as if the story was telling itself.

I hope you enjoy reading this book as much as I enjoyed writing it. Please visit me at www.lisaruff.net. And keep a watch out for my next book from Harlequin.

Happy reading,

Lisa Ruff

Man of the Year
LISA RUFF

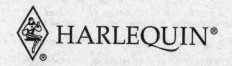

HARLEQUIN®

TORONTO • NEW YORK • LONDON
AMSTERDAM • PARIS • SYDNEY • HAMBURG
STOCKHOLM • ATHENS • TOKYO • MILAN • MADRID
PRAGUE • WARSAW • BUDAPEST • AUCKLAND

ISBN-13: 978-0-373-75218-8
ISBN-10: 0-373-75218-0

MAN OF THE YEAR

www.eHarlequin.com

Printed in U.S.A.

ABOUT THE AUTHOR

Lisa Ruff was born in Montana and grew up in Idaho but met the man of her dreams in Seattle. She married Kirk promising to love, honor and edit his rough drafts. His pursuit of writing led Lisa to the craft. A longtime reader of romance, she decided to try to create one herself. The first version of *Man of the Year* took three months to finish, but her day job got in the way of polishing the manuscript. She stuffed it into a drawer, where it languished for several years.

In pursuit of time to write and freedom to explore the world, Lisa, Kirk and their cat sailed from Seattle on a thirty-seven-foot boat. They spent five years cruising around Central America and the Caribbean. Lisa wrote romance, but it took a backseat to an adventurous life. She was busy writing travel essays, learning to speak Spanish from taxi drivers and handling a small boat in gale-force winds.

When she returned to land life, she finally revised *Man of the Year* and sent it to an agent. Within a year she had a contract from Harlequin American Romance.

She and her husband are cruising on a sailboat again somewhere in the Atlantic Ocean. When not setting sail for another port, she is working on her next Harlequin romance.

For Kirk.
I could not have done it without you.
Thanks for giving up Maine.

Chapter One

Samantha took a deep breath and unclenched her fists as she neared the wide blue doors. *Relax, it's just another job.* But this was not just another job, at least not like any others she'd had. The doors were closed, but the scent of the locker room slipped past them and wafted around her. Male sweat, liniment and antifungal remedies teased her nose, growing stronger with each step. At the doors, her guide, Peter Brinks, stopped and cleared his throat.

"Here we are."

She answered with a smile she hoped showed cool assurance. Beyond these doors was a male sanctuary where few women ventured. Few were allowed. Samantha was one of the lucky ones. Or unlucky, depending on how things went today. The thought made her fists clench again. She chided herself: it was only a locker room—no big deal. She had seen a man naked before, right? This was her job and going in there was part of the deal. She squared her shoulders and uncurled her fingers, but sweat coated her palms. She had to admit the truth to herself: an entire *room* full of naked men was a daunting prospect.

Peter opened one of the doors and poked his head inside. "Hey, guys. Cover up," he yelled in warning. "I got a lady coming through."

The laughter and chatter swelling out of the room ebbed for a moment. Peter waited, his head still around the edge of the blue door. Samantha smothered a laugh. He was as nervous as she was about all those naked bodies she might glimpse. Finally, he stood back, opening the door wide for her.

"Everything looks decent in there now, Miss James." Peter chuckled as he ushered her through the door. "At least as decent as it gets in this place. Right this way."

Peter led her through a maze of wood benches and metal lockers enameled the same shade of blue as the two front doors. A fine mist hung in the room, courtesy of the hot showers, and the smells were even more pungent inside. The wintergreen of liniment combined with acrid sweat made Samantha's eyes sting. She tried not to stare as she passed the athletes in various states of undress. It was not easy. They were so large and…and muscular. The steam from the showers glistened on rippling biceps and washboard stomachs. Drops of water slipped down powerful chests and into the curling hair spread there. It was no different from being at the beach, she told herself. But she knew that was a lie. These men were professional athletes. They were paid— and paid well—to keep their bodies in top condition. Her uncontrollable fascination embarrassed her, though not enough to stop her from sneaking glances. This was better than any beach she had ever visited.

The men watched her pass through their midst with just as much curiosity—and, it seemed to her in some cases, with as much embarrassment. After all, it wasn't every day that a woman strolled through this male domain. But Samantha expected to spend much more time here in the future, so they had better get used to her. She would have to get used to them, too. Peter led the way through the maze of maleness to a glass-walled office on one side. As she followed him into it, Samantha's attention settled on the matter at hand. She widened her smile and stuck her hand out confidently.

"Coach Cummings, I'm Samantha James. It's a pleasure to meet you."

JARRETT CORLISS WAS ONE of forty players that watched the woman weave through the room. Unlike some of his teammates, he was not embarrassed to be clad in only a damp towel, slung low across his hips, while a beautiful woman walked past. He was curious, though. The slim, graceful redhead had caused a hush to fall over the normally raucous room. More than one head had swiveled to follow the gently swaying hips beneath the navy-blue suit. And since they were looking in that general direction, they gave her legs a thorough assessment, too: long, luxurious legs encased in silk that looked like they lasted forever.

The fiery mane of hair wrapped into a neat roll at the base of her neck caught Jarrett's eye first. He scanned down the rest of her body and back to her face, where his attention locked. From across the room he could see her straight nose, arched eyebrows and clear, peachy skin. What color were her eyes? They must be green to set off that hair. Jarrett narrowed his eyes, squinting as he did during his wind up on the mound. What would she look like without the stiff business suit, he wondered. Just how far did that peachy skin go?

Jarrett absently rubbed his right shoulder, running his hand over the ridge of scar tissue as he stared at her back. And just how did a woman like that fit into management's plans? With all the changes around the club, he wouldn't be surprised to see them walk an elephant through this place. A woman made him more wary. He rubbed his shoulder harder and figured he would find out soon enough.

"Shoulder bothering you, Corliss?"

Jarrett turned to the pitching coach. "It's a little stiff. A few more workouts, it'll be fit as a fiddle," he replied with a sure wink.

The coach didn't smile in return. "Give it a good soaking in the whirlpool. And don't overwork it." Before Jarrett could answer, the coach was interrogating another pitcher.

Jarrett grimaced. Was the guy joking? As if he would take chances at this stage of recovery. He tried not to let the burning in his shoulder affect his temper, but the coach's trite advice, coupled with the annoying pain in the joint, ate at him. There was not one inning, not one single practice, when someone wasn't doubting him or fretting over his pitching or his shoulder. Well, let them worry. The satisfaction of proving them all wrong in the end would be worth the pain now.

In his better moments, Jarrett understood why everyone was skeptical. He could be as realistic as they were. Maybe more so. Few teams wanted to take a chance on a pitcher recovering from rotator-cuff surgery. When the injured pitcher was already twenty-eight years old and there were dozens of other hungry, younger arms begging for a chance, why bother with a has-been? But Jarrett had recovered, or at least he was on his way. He had proved himself a few times in practice this last week, so the coach's fussing irked him. It also spurred him to work harder, to put more speed in his fastball, more curve in his slider, for himself and for the team. Mostly for himself. The Rainiers were his last hope.

And if the Rainiers were his last hope, he was theirs, too. The team was in deep trouble. Management denied it fervently to the sports reporters and even to the players, but a persistent rumor said the team would be sold before the end of the season and moved to some other city. He rubbed his shoulder again.

Jarrett knew the Rainiers' troubles were precisely the reason they had plucked him as a last-chance free agent. The team's owner, Andrew Elliott, needed a winning season, but couldn't afford the best pitcher in the world. He also didn't have time to groom a new pitcher. So like any desperate owner strapped for cash, Elliott had gone bargain hunting and found Jarrett, injured but full of potential, experience and skill. So while Jarrett was not exactly the Rainiers' best hope, he was the best hope they could afford. He was realistic about this. Even grateful. They were taking a chance on him. He would give them everything he had, which might be a considerable contribution if his shoulder held up. And if not? Well, best not to think of that.

Coach Cummings blew a short, sharp blast on the whistle that always hung around his neck. Every head snapped to attention, including Jarrett's. Alongside the coach stood the peachy-skinned redhead.

"Men, I want to introduce Samantha James. She's with Emerald Advertising. The club has hired her and her company to promote our team and maybe get a few more citizens into the stadium when we take the field." All eyes that weren't on her already shifted to look at Samantha. No one bothered looking at the coach again. "I'm going to bring her around and introduce her. She would like to speak with each of you personally, since—"

"Honey, you can get as personal with me as you'd like," a voice called out from the back of the room. The remark was accompanied by a loud snap that could only have come from the elastic of a jockstrap. The words and the snap brought a burst of laughter from the rest of the team.

Jarrett watched to see how the redhead, Samantha, took the teasing. He thought she would either wither and crawl under a rock, or storm out and threaten to sue the whole bunch of them for sexual harassment. He saw her crane her long, slender neck to find the perpetrator.

"Well, *honey,*" she said, a faint smile on her lips, "the first thing I'm looking for is a spokesman in a TV commercial. A really *loud* one. You might just get the part."

This comment raised another round of laughter. The redhead gave as good as she got, without ruffling any feathers. Jarrett's admiration reluctantly rose a few notches. Sexy as sin and a sense of humor: the woman might be dangerous.

"All right, listen up!" the coach yelled over the raucous banter and hooting that had resumed. He paused for a fierce glare at the players. "As I was saying before I was interrupted, Ms. James would like to meet all of you—God only knows why. So cooperate with her and try to act your best for a change." As soon as the coach finished speaking, the noise in the locker room went back to its previous high decibels.

Jarrett watched discreetly as Samantha moved from one player to the next. The coach performed introductions. She seemed to be joking with each guy, if the smiles and laughter were any indication. She was even getting along with the worst chauvinists on the team. Such a sweet little thing, she was. Pretty as the dew on a honeysuckle vine, as his daddy in Oklahoma would say. Too bad sweet things got chewed up and eaten in this locker room.

She and Coach Cummings circled the room, starting at its far end. With each handshake and burst of small talk, those long, gorgeous legs took one more step toward Jarrett. He had to admire her poise. The only woman in the room, she seemed indifferent to the state of dress—or undress—of the men with whom she shook hands and talked. He glanced at his own towel and decided to leave it. Besides, he couldn't very well drop it to the floor with her in the room. Or could he?

SAMANTHA PUT ON HER best business smile and gave each player a firm, confident handshake. She asked questions, tried to remember each name and laughed where appropriate. All the while, her head swirled with ideas for an ad campaign. Each man put on a show for her benefit, unknowingly fueling her creative process. Teasing comments flew, but they were never aimed directly at her. Their quips were saved for one another, each one trying to insult the other better than he had been insulted. Their jokes told her volumes about each man. Her anxiety had nearly disappeared, and she began to worry less about being the only woman here as her hope grew. This might not be such an impossible job after all. With the right hook, a good spin and a few flashy graphics, the public would love every single player—even if they didn't think much of the whole team.

The Rainiers were a challenge for any advertising firm. With a string of losses and a host of scandals, their public image was at rock bottom. Before meeting these men, when she had first won the dubious honor of promoting them, she had wondered about the chances of increasing ticket sales. And her own chances at helping them do it. Now before her was a room full of boys pretending to be professional athletes. It was comical, even touching. They wanted so much to be liked, respected and admired. It seemed hopeless. Yet she had to come up with an idea that would capture the very jaded hearts of former fans and regain some of their lost loyalty. The Rainiers' future was at stake. So was hers and her company's.

Her mind wandered off on another tangent. Maybe she could use the idea about little boys playing baseball. It would make a cute, humorous TV spot, something endearing that would show their innocent, earnest side. While considering this, she found herself standing before a tall man. He was clad only in a towel, which draped around his lean hips precariously. That towel drew her eyes as well as her imagination. She stopped thinking about the appeal of little boys in TV commercials and started considering other appealing possibilities. As she stared at the towel, the tall man reached down and tightened the damp cloth to fit more snugly. The white terrycloth barely left enough room for her imagination to work.

"Samantha, this is Jarrett Corliss." Coach Cummings's voice reached her ears dimly. "He's a pitcher, one of our starters this season."

"Pleased to meet you, Samantha." His voice was deep and mellow, with more than a hint of a sweet, country drawl.

His hand reached out, and she unconsciously met it with her own. Samantha barely heard someone call to the coach from across the room, telling him that he was wanted on the telephone. The coach excused himself, but it was as if he had ceased to exist already. Everyone had. For Samantha, the steamy locker room had emptied except for her and this man in front of her. Her eyes crawled upward from the white towel, over the flat, tautly muscled belly to the broad chest scattered with curly, dark-blond hair. The corded neck and shoulders invited her touch.

Her gaze went farther up and finally met a pair of eyes. They dazzled her with the blue of a summer sky over a wide, endless prairie. The eyes were set in a sun-bronzed face, and a wave of hair the color of corn silk dipped over one arched brow. A dimple flashed beside the sculpted lips. The eyes had followed her deliberate stare as she made her way from the towel to look directly into them. Now those blue eyes twinkled with unabashed amusement.

Without a word, the man—she had forgotten his name already—took the same liberty. He was in no hurry, either. His gaze traveled slowly from the top of her head, down across her breasts, her legs and back to her face. She felt a prickling sensation on her skin where his eyes touched. She bridled at being gazed at so intensely and deliberately—never mind that she had committed the same crime just seconds ago.

Samantha struggled to retain her professional demeanor. Why did this man in a towel affect her so much more than the other half-dressed men? By now the clasp of their hands had strayed far from a polite greeting into something more intimate and dangerous. Realizing she was holding his hand, not shaking it, Samantha pulled back abruptly.

"Well." Her tone was husky, reaching for brisk firmness and failing. "It's nice to meet you as well, Mr.—" she said, fumbling for his name.

"Jarrett. Jarrett Corliss."

"Right. Mr. Corliss."

"Just Jarrett," he interrupted before she could say any more. "*Mr.* Corliss is in Oklahoma getting ready for this season's crop of peppers and tomatoes." A slow grin came to his lips. "I always thought Dad had it bad, sittin' on a tractor all day in the sun. But standin' around in a towel meeting beautiful women is a whole lot hotter and sweatier work than plowin' up a field."

His voice had lowered, and the words steamed in Samantha's ears, hot with meaning and suggestion. His eyes were trained on hers. Their laughing sparkle invited her to share the joke. She could feel the heat—the heat that came from their blue depths as much as his bare torso.

"If it's that unpleasant in here, you ought to take a nice cold shower," she suggested. Samantha stepped back a pace, but he moved with her. He was deliberately trying to throw her off balance.

"And take off my towel?" His glance flickered over her once more in swift appraisal. "Is that what you want?"

Samantha got a grip on herself. Her immediate attraction to this man's physical presence was undeniable. She felt it down to her bones. But she didn't intend to let that get in the way of her job. She smiled coolly.

"It would be a fabulous publicity shot. But not suitable for our target market." Before he could take her up on the offer to pose naked, she changed the subject abruptly. "So, you're the new kid on the mound."

"Yes, ma'am. And real eager to work closely with you on publicity. *Very* close." Jarrett's lips curved into a smile that deepened the beautiful, mischievous dimple in his left cheek.

Samantha almost smiled at his persistent charm. His wide grin told her that he read her amusement. She ignored it and said crisply, "Good. We'll need everyone's cooperation."

"Well, you let me know when and where you want me to cooperate, Samantha," he drawled. "I'll come runnin'."

Whatever she might have said next was interrupted when a muscular arm suddenly dropped over her shoulders. Then a whisker-stubbled face smacked a kiss on her cheek.

"Sammy, what's a nice girl like you doing in a dump like this?"

JARRETT WATCHED IN AMAZEMENT as the left fielder, the biggest, most obnoxious womanizer on the team, swooped down on Samantha and kissed her. Jarrett's lips tightened as irritation washed through him. Boomer—nicknamed that because of his power hitting—was a jerk and here he was hanging all over this gorgeous woman. Jarrett silently cursed him.

He had been making progress with Samantha. Despite her cool replies to his bantering, she was attracted. There was nothing cool in her green eyes when she looked at him. They had burned his naked skin wherever they touched. She liked what she saw. Hell, if he ever got the chance to look at her wearing only a towel, he wouldn't pass it up, either. Now Boomer had blown everything.

"So you had to make a personal appearance, Sammy,"

Boomer teased. "What? Don't you trust any of your flunkies to do the job?"

"Oh, I trust my *employees*. It's you and your little friends here that I have misgivings about."

Their banter was comfortable—*familiar*. Obviously, they knew each other well. They might not be doing this chummy routine to aggravate him, but that was the result. Jarrett ground his teeth. He watched with annoyance—and no small amount of envy—as Boomer curved an arm around Samantha's waist, and gave it an affectionate squeeze.

"Yeah, you may not trust me, but you gotta love me anyway." He gave Samantha another bold, bristly kiss, then turned to Jarrett. "Hey, Jarry. How's the ol' shoulder holding out? I hear you might have to pitch underhanded."

Jarrett crossed his arms over his chest. Boomer thought himself a great comedian. "It's fine. How's your ol' arm doing?"

"Great. Never felt better," the left fielder replied and flexed the biceps in his free arm. "I've been knocking them out of the park." Boomer turned his attention back to Samantha again. "Listen, Sammy, have you got a minute? I need to talk."

"About what?"

Boomer flashed a glance at Jarrett. "Not now, you're too busy. How about later, when you're done here?"

Samantha's curiosity was evident. "All right. I'll try to catch up with you after I've finished."

"Great!"

Boomer pressed another kiss on her cheek and walked away with a parting wave. Jarrett noticed how Samantha's eyes followed him out the door.

"Known him long?" The question rushed out before he could stop it.

"Since we were in diapers," she quipped. She wore a

generous, teasing smile, as if she knew that this vague information would really goad him.

"I guess 'Sammy' comes from a long way back, too." Jarrett tried to sound politely interested. To his ears, he failed miserably. He was surprised to see Samantha's cheeks tint lightly in a rosy blush.

"Yes, it does. But you can call me Samantha."

"Sure," he muttered under his breath. "For now."

Coach Cummings rejoined them, forestalling any further retort from Jarrett. "Sorry about that, Ms. James. That was Mr. Elliott. I see you've had more than enough time to size up Jarrett."

"Yes, thanks, Coach. Mr. Corliss and I are finished."

"He's the last rat in the pack. Now, you wanted to take a look at the uniforms?"

"Yes, then the stadium."

"Sure. Follow me."

Before the coach escorted her away, Jarrett summoned a grin and winked at her. Boomer was gone and that was reason enough to smile. "It's truly been a pleasure, Samantha. Call me when you need help with your sales pitch. Pitching's what I do best."

Her eyes flickered to his, but she looked away before he could catch a hint of her thoughts. She didn't say another word, just walked out with the coach. Jarrett watched her until she was gone. *You may be finished with me,* he thought, *but I'm not finished with you. Not by a long shot.*

SAMANTHA FELT JARRETT'S EYES follow her every step out of the locker room. As the coach showed her the team uniforms, the costume for the mascot—a brown fuzzy suit that was supposed to resemble a marmot, but looked more like a man-sized rug—and gave her a tour of the stadium, she mused over Jarrett Corliss. Like most jocks, he obviously thought of himself as God's gift to women. With his teasing blue eyes and that dimple, she supposed he had more than his fair share of baseball groupies. He would be popular with the young women who hung around the gates after practice or a game, offering their bodies to anything in a uniform. "Mitt-muffins," Boomer called them. Jarrett probably took advantage of that willingness on occasion, too. Just like all the other players.

Samantha had yet to meet a baseball jock who would resist what a mitt-muffin offered. She supposed they saw it as their due, a perk of fame and success. But, to her, it was repugnant. She had tried to love a ballplayer once or twice and learned a bitter lesson. Let the boys have their fun: she would find a real man who played the game by the rules.

Which made her own starstruck gawking at Jarrett doubly embarrassing. What had she been thinking? She had acted like a groupie—or nearly as bad. No wonder he had flirted with her so outrageously. He was gorgeous, she admitted, but he was just one piece of her advertising campaign. Nothing more, nothing less. This was business, not some singles club. From now on, she would treat him like all the rest of the team. She would put his offer of cooperation to profitable use—though certainly not the way *he* intended.

She pushed Jarrett Corliss and his dimples to the back of her mind and concentrated on the tour Coach Cummings was giving her. She took copious notes as they walked to the dugout, stood at home plate and took a quick tour of the concessions area. Every new sight, every detail, added to the ideas swirling in her head. All the while, she peppered the coach with questions. When they completed the tour and the talk, Samantha had a feel for the inner workings of the Rainiers: how they practiced, who made decisions on and off the field, what they hoped to achieve and how, and what the biggest obstacles were to winning. She requested videotapes of recent practices and last year's games. Cummings promised that he would get them to her office before the week's end.

By the time they were finished with their tour, the team had dispersed from the locker room. Peter Brinks told her that Boomer had also left for the day. Whatever her brother had to say must not be that important. She bid goodbye to Coach Cummings and slipped through the wire-mesh gate to the parking lot.

The chilly wind and rain cut through her wool suit and she was glad to get inside her red BMW. She turned the heater up full blast and used the wipers to flick away the light mist on the windshield. The typical late-January weather made her long for spring. She skirted Pioneer Square, empty of the tourists that would flock there in summer. She loved this part of Seattle, the buildings all graceful relics of the past. Her car crossed Yesler Avenue, the original "Skid Row" where logs had been skidded down to the water, milled and shipped away to provide lumber for the world. As she drove, she puzzled over her encounter with Jarrett Corliss. Why had she been so taken in? The way he looked in a towel was undeniably sexy. What woman wouldn't think so? But she ought to know better.

While stopped at a red light, the idea suddenly hit her. Of course! It was the perfect way to get people back into the stadium: sex appeal. She would scatter one or two good photos of the pitcher in tight jeans or a well-tailored Rainiers uniform around town on billboards or in the local magazines. Women would come in droves to see him. Some of his teammates might have the same sex appeal. She knew her little brother would love the idea of strutting his stuff for the camera. Fill the ballpark with women, and the men would quickly follow. The picture of Jarrett wrapped in a towel merged with the players acting like little boys. Pieces of a commercial started to fall into place in her head. The light turned green. Samantha hit the accelerator and sped toward her office.

Chapter Two

Samantha rushed in out of the rain and walked briskly to the elevator. The brass hand in an arch above the doors pointed at the number ten, slowly dropped to nine, then stopped. She waited, staring at the ornate brass curlicues on the door in front of her without actually seeing them. Her mind was still on the commercial for the Rainiers. A few minutes later a soft chime sounded, and the doors opened. An old man in a burgundy uniform with gold braid carefully held the door for her to enter.

"Hello, Ted."

"Good afternoon, Miss James. A fine day we've got, don't you think?"

Samantha grinned at the elevator operator. "With rain and wind like this, you can say it's a fine day?"

"Oh, well, it's Seattle. If this isn't a fine day, then it'll be a while before we have one."

Samantha laughed. He was right. With all the rain in Seattle, they had to appreciate days when it only drizzled. Ted pulled the door closed and shifted the lever to "up." With a clank and a slight wheeze, the ancient elevator rose slowly to the twelfth floor. The Smith Tower, the oldest high-rise in the city, had its quirks. This elegant brass relic of an elevator was one of them. But Samantha loved the old building. Much taller skyscrapers rose all around, but they seemed like polished, characterless monoliths in comparison. Since 1913, the tower had outlasted both developers that coveted the land it occupied and earthquakes that tried to shake it down. Now, quirks and all, it was an intrinsic part of the Seattle skyline. It was also the perfect home for Samantha's company.

The car jerked to a halt, a foot above the twelfth floor. Ted patiently shifted the lever up and down, joggling the car closer to the same level as the floor. Samantha waited just as patiently, though she would have been happy to hop down the short distance. The elevator was Ted's pride and joy, and Samantha respected his need to do his job perfectly. He opened the brass gate and waved Samantha on her way.

"Thanks, Ted."

"My pleasure, Miss James. You have a good day."

Walking down the short hall, Samantha opened the door into her corner of the advertising world. On the front end, Emerald Advertising looked like any other business. Muted rose paint on the walls and furniture upholstered in navy and plum greeted the visitor, an image of tasteful yet understated affluence. At the large mahogany reception desk, phones rang quietly and were answered graciously. The lighting was also subdued, soft. Two equally inviting conference rooms, one large and one small, lay directly behind the reception area.

If Samantha knew anything about her business, it was that packaging made the product. Her clients had preconceived ideas of how a successful ad business should look, how it felt, smelled and worked. So, she gave them glass walls, a touch of brass and chairs with ample padding: the plush trappings where deals could be made in comfort. The front office looked spacious and gracious, as Samantha liked to say, with enough room to stretch out your checkbook.

Behind this formal front lurked Emerald Advertising's messier, creative side. A three-quarter-height wall of frosted glass separated one half from the other. Occasionally, this seamier side of the company slipped over the wall and broke into the respectable realm. While sitting in the waiting area, clients occasionally caught glimpses of objects flying through the air. These strange sights happened so suddenly that they were usually dismissed as figments of the imagination—indoor UFOs. After all, mature adults did not throw things in an office, did they?

Samantha greeted the receptionist. Debbie smoothly put one caller on hold while simultaneously routing another call back to Pam at her desk.

"Brenda pulled your messages when she got back from lunch. I've put most of your calls through to her this afternoon."

Samantha thanked her and walked behind the wall into "Never-Never Land" as her employees called it. Most of the back half of the business had no walls, cubicles or other hindrances to carve up the space. Only Samantha's corner office was enclosed. The walls were frosted glass for an illusion of privacy, but her door was nearly always open. Illustrators and copywriters were free to toss ideas back and forth—or erasers, spitballs or rubber bands, if the whims of creativity so required it. The front office decor flowed back to this area, but in a more lively fashion. Where the entrance to Emerald Advertising inspired business, the working area inspired creativity. The colors were bolder and brighter, the energy level higher.

The clutter in this creative room was terrible, which was mostly Samantha's fault. She encouraged her employees to hang personal art, current projects, comic strips on the walls—anything pertinent to their work, and things not so pertinent, whatever generated fresh ideas and imaginative thoughts. It was an idea factory where slogans, logos and images for products from detergent to auto parts were crafted. The waste from this process littered the tables, desks and floor.

One of four walls was entirely devoted to Emerald's competition. Ads for lingerie, espresso, software, oil-and-lube service and more were plastered one atop another. Comments were scribbled across them. Just above eye level to the left was a small banner that read Worst. To the far right was a similar banner with Best. Under these headings were the ads that had won either award that week. For each ad pinned to the wall, Samantha wanted a critique. Did it succeed in promoting the product? Why did it fail? How could Emerald do it differently? How would they do it better?

Better was always what Samantha wanted from her company, her employees and herself. Because of this, Emerald Advertising had earned a steadily increasing reputation for fresh, offbeat campaigns in the marketing world. It was a reputation that Samantha worked hard to cultivate. Staying on the cutting edge of advertising was a continual challenge. That's what made the work so interesting. In time, Samantha hoped to turn Emerald into one of the leading advertising firms in the city—and the nation. The contract with the Seattle Rainiers was a critical step toward fulfilling that dream.

She stopped to greet Stuart and Lane, one of her best creative teams.

"How's it going, guys?"

"Pretty good, Ms. Boss-lady," Lane answered playfully. "We've got the storyboards ready for Big Snot Auto Parts. I think they'll go for it."

Samantha laughed at Lane's irreverence. "Good. When do you meet with them?"

Stuart answered. "Next Tuesday."

"I'd like to see what you've got planned." Samantha

glanced at the clock. "Not this afternoon. How about first thing tomorrow morning?"

The two men agreed, and Samantha moved on to her office. She smiled, thinking about Stuart and Lane. As a creative team, they worked together beautifully, though she sometimes thought that they shared the same mind. Often you'd ask a question of one, and the other would answer. Or one would finish the sentence that the other had started. Nice guys, but odd—perfect for advertising and her company.

As she went through the door to her office, Samantha noticed a short, blond spike of hair peeking over the top of her blue swivel chair. Those pale spikes could only belong to Brenda Miller, Samantha's right-hand woman. Brenda kept Samantha's world organized. She followed the progress of current projects, passed on the information she thought needed to be heard, and filed the rest for future use. Samantha was certain Brenda could do at least seven things at once. Besides all that, Brenda was Samantha's closest friend.

"Hey, what is this? Some sort of coup?" Samantha teased. "I'm gone for two hours, and you've already taken over."

"Samantha!" Brenda spun around in her boss's chair, ignoring her teasing. "How did everything go? Did you meet the team?"

The question was laced with more excitement and zest than Brenda usually mustered for business. She and her husband, Craig, a lawyer, were dedicated Rainiers fans. She had made Samantha promise that she would get autographs of any new players for Brenda's collection.

"It was fine." Samantha dropped her briefcase to the floor and perched on the edge of the desk, flipping through the mail piled on it.

"Come *on,* Samantha," Brenda begged. "Fine can*not* describe a trip to a locker room full of half-naked, gorgeous hunks of male flesh."

Samantha laughed. "Why do you think they were half-naked?"

"Wishful thinking."

Samantha chuckled at Brenda's wistful look. "Well, I *might* have noticed one or two that were wearing less than the regulation uniform." An image of Jarrett Corliss wrapped in a damp towel popped into her mind, as if it were a jack-in-the-box that had wound itself up, springing into her head unannounced. Samantha blinked, pushed the image back into the box and slammed the lid tight.

"What do you mean? Or should I say *who* do you mean?"

"No one," Samantha denied firmly.

"Bull. You met someone."

Samantha shook her head. "I'll tell you later. What's happened here at the factory?"

Brenda allowed the subject change without comment. "Running wild and crazy as usual. If there are any problems, everyone seems to be handling them on their own and not sharing them with me." She levered herself out of Samantha's chair with some effort. "Boy, that gets harder to do every day."

Samantha reached out and helped her friend to her feet, steadied her, then patted the protruding stomach. Six months pregnant, Brenda had started to waddle a bit. "Junior giving you problems today?"

"Only when he does a tap dance on my bladder." She sighed. "Now, the urgent mail is on the left, the not-so-urgent is on the right, the important messages are here, I fielded the rest. You want a cup of coffee?"

"I can get one myself. I thought the smell made you nauseous." Samantha sat and looked over the piles Brenda had indicated.

"Not anymore," Brenda said with a grimace. "Now cat food, *that* makes me green." Both women laughed at that.

"Then, yes, thank you. I'd love a cup. And if you've got time, I'd like to go over the material I picked up at the Rainiers today. I think I have a campaign just about figured out."

"Jeez, you're quick. Stuart and Lane will be disappointed. They want to come up with all the brilliant ideas."

Samantha wiggled her eyebrows and did a poor imitation of Groucho Marx. "I had a lot of inspiration while I was there."

Brenda groaned. "Okay, I'll get my notepad and the coffee and be right back."

Samantha pulled a thick file from her briefcase. She took an envelope of photographs from the file and went to the large worktable just outside her office door. Around her, activity buzzed. Stuart and Lane took turns shooting a foam basketball through a hoop over the windows. Samantha didn't ask what that had to do with auto parts. A printer hummed, spitting out paper. Carol hunched over a computer, composing a layout. Somewhere in the back Pam argued on the phone.

Samantha spread the photographs out before her on the table. Eight-by-ten headshots mingled with the "action" poses that she had always found corny. She pulled out the headshots and lined them across the table. Players were identified by name across the bottom of each photo. Other personal data, vital statistics and averages were listed on the back. None of the official information said much about the individuals. Samantha recalled her conversations with the players: their jokes, their quirks, their stories all came back to her.

"So this is the new team." Brenda peeked over Samantha's shoulder. "Here's your coffee."

"Thanks."

"Not bad." Brenda picked up a photo. "Hey, this is José Alvendia. He used to play for Houston. Craig and I wondered what had happened to him. He used to be really good."

"Let's hope he's still really good." Samantha eyed the photo.

"Between you and me, Elliott told me that this is the last chance he's giving the team. If they don't turn things around, he's going to sell it."

"What? I thought the city had a contract with him for two years."

"No, only one year is guaranteed. The second year depends on this season's revenues."

"You think they can do it? Pull the club out of the toilet, I mean?" Brenda knew as much or more about the team as anyone, and the skepticism was evident in her tone.

"I don't know. Elliott's put some money into getting players. About half of these guys are new this year." Samantha waved at the spread of photos with her coffee cup. "But your guess is as good as anyone's whether they can pull it off."

"Well, that could either mean new energy, or too many egos to make a team work together."

"Exactly." Samantha sipped her coffee thoughtfully. "But for better or worse, we've got to shove our personal doubts aside and assume they'll succeed."

Brenda eased herself onto a chair at the side of the table. "Maybe we should just stick to auto parts and bookstores."

Samantha eyed the photos as she pondered Brenda's words. Not only had the Rainiers been rock-bottom in the league, they'd also managed to bring just about every scandal swirling around the club: drugs, drunk driving, bar fights. One player had even been caught having an affair with the mayor's wife.

"Well, at least the problem players have either been suspended indefinitely or left the team," Samantha said, thinking aloud.

"Or they're in jail."

"Don't remind me. It's been four months since the end of last season. If we hit the public with a whole new image, play up the bright future the team has, I think we can win the fans over."

"So what's your big idea, boss?" Brenda sipped the glass of water she held. "How's the rookie ad-lady going to save the day?"

Samantha perched on the edge of the table, facing Brenda. "Try this one: When I was talking with some of the players, I had this flashback to grade school. Do you remember at recess, the boys would try to outdo one another with jokes and tricks when they were around the girls? They'd do all this silly stuff just to get our attention and we ended up thinking they were just that—silly?"

"Yeah, and the weirdest ones always turned out to be the guys you dated in high school," Brenda said with a laugh. "So how does this sell a baseball team?"

"What if we play on that image to reintroduce the team to the public? Especially the new ones. Set up a series of commercials with the players shown as boys. Take them through childhood when they're on the playground to adulthood in the stadium. Each guy would have some particular talent that revealed itself at an early age. Or maybe it's just a quirk that has followed him through life that makes him good at what he does now."

"You mean like the naughty boy throwing a rock that breaks a church window?" Brenda asked. "In the next spot, he's the team's star pitcher."

"Exactly. That's a good one."

"What about the print ads and the billboards?"

"We could use stills of each player, showing a parody of them as a kid, then as an adult. You know, a photo of a kid breaking the church window, then a still of the actual player winding up for a pitch." Samantha felt the seed of the idea blossoming in her head. "We can use the new faces on the team. The old ones, too. Introduce all of them so it's like there's a completely new ball club. We give the customer the feeling of getting to know the team from day one. How a new era of great baseball got started. Or, at least a new season." Samantha finished with a shrug.

Brenda sat for a moment sipping her water. "This has promise, boss. You're good. But I'm still thinking about those half-naked men. What about them?"

"What half-naked men?"

"The half-naked men that gave you that glazed look a little while ago? You said you'd explain later. It's later now." Brenda was watching Samantha with wide, guileless eyes.

Samantha was not fooled. "Hmm. Think you're pretty smart, don't you?"

"That's why you hired me."

"I haven't quite figured out where the half-naked men fit into the picture, but I have my target."

"Who?"

"Jarrett Corliss."

"The pitcher with the bum shoulder? Why him?"

Samantha sorted through the photos and pulled one from the mess. "This is why." She handed it to Brenda.

Brenda took one look at the blond, blue-cyed man and whistled her approval. "My, oh my. He was with Arizona a while ago, wasn't he? I wondered what happened to him." Brenda shot an inquiring look at Samantha, then added, "Well, his shoulder may be toast, but the rest of him has sure improved with age."

"Brenda, I am telling you the complete and honest truth— this man is the best-looking thing in a damp towel that I've *ever* seen in all my twenty-eight years." Samantha pointed her finger at the other woman. "And that opinion is never to be mentioned outside of this conversation."

Brenda had a steadily widening grin on her face. "That good, huh? He's the reason for your glazed, dreamy look?"

Samantha had to smile. "Well, he did kind of…pop into my head unexpectedly."

The two burst into laughter that had a decidedly wicked ring to it. Others in the office glanced up to see what the joke was, then went back to what they were doing after deciding that it was private.

Samantha wiped the corner of her eyes. "He's also the…what do I want to say? He's the *smoothest* man I've ever met." She felt her blood sizzle from the memory of Jarrett's bold appraisal. "He's from somewhere south—"

"Oklahoma," Brenda supplied, looking at the back of the photo she held.

"Oklahoma, then. He has a drawl and entirely more charm than what's good for him."

Brenda laughed. "Sounds like you've got a thing for the man in the towel."

"No way, Bren. No ballplayers. *Never* again. You know that."

"It's been a long time, Samantha." Brenda looked at her friend directly. "Just because he plays baseball, doesn't mean he's going to run around on you."

"Whether he plays baseball or not, he's not going to get the chance."

Brenda shot her an exasperated look. "Those were *boys*, Sam. These—" she waved a hand at the photos arrayed on the table "—are men who know what mitt-muffins are like and what they want. Not *every* guy in the league is only interested in empty sex."

Samantha snorted. "Yeah, and I'm the Queen of Sheba. The mitt-muffins are just the tip of the iceberg, Bren. It's the ego I can't stand. Every player I ever met acted like he's God's gift to the universe. That hasn't changed much from when I was a kid, hanging out at Boomer's high school games." Samantha looked at Jarrett's picture, then turned it so the handsome smile was directed at Brenda. "This guy's got an ego as big as them all. Maybe bigger."

"You know that after meeting him just once?"

"Oh, yeah, that came through loud and clear."

"But he still turned you on," Brenda added smugly.

"I said he was sexy, not that I was interested in him."

"I say *go* for it, Sam. If he's as sexy as you—"

"You know I can't, even if I *did* want to," Samantha interrupted. "I told you what Elliott said."

"He can't tell you who you can and can't date," Brenda said.

"Sure he can. He holds all the cards. At least as far as the team is concerned."

"You think he'd cancel the contract because you went on a *date* with a player?" Brenda was incredulous.

"I don't know if he would cancel, but he could make our lives very difficult," Samantha said, serious now. "I can't—I won't—take the risk of finding out how far he's willing to be pushed. I *do* know Elliott was dead serious when he said he didn't want any trace of scandal around the team."

"I suppose you're right." Brenda sounded doubtful.

"I know I am. We need this contract much more than I need a date with some smooth-talking, sexy farm boy from Oklahoma."

"It's your call, Sam."

"Exactly, and I don't want anything that smells even vaguely suspicious getting back to Elliott's nose. Besides, I get enough of baseball from Boomer. More, I don't need."

"Speaking of which, what are you going to do about him?" Brenda shuffled the pictures and came up with Boomer's. "What's his bit in all this?"

"Nothing special. I treat him just like any other player. He knows that and so do I. Elliott didn't seem to think there was a problem, as long as we both knew that there would be no special treatment. I told him about the connection, but it turns out he already knew. Thanks to Boomer."

"He told him?" Brenda asked, surprised. "Why would he do that?"

"Little brother didn't want any blotch on his career because I was bidding on the team's ad contract."

"Huh? I don't get it."

Samantha shrugged. "That's how he explained it. As it turned out, I may have gotten the contract because of my connection with him, at least indirectly. Elliott said that my knowledge of baseball was one thing that tipped the scale in our favor."

"That and being low bidder."

"Well, his budget is tight this year, so that worked to our advantage as well."

Samantha was philosophical about why she had beaten other, more prestigious firms for the high-profile job. In the end, all that mattered was that she knew her team could do the work as well as, or better than, any other firm. She had convinced Elliott of that. And her spiel to him was not merely boastful, hopeful words. Samantha would not have taken the contract if she did not think Emerald was right for the job and that the job was right for Emerald.

The size of the project was a bit daunting for a small company, though. The firm would be responsible for not only the advertising, but also a new logo, uniform design and colors. Caps, buttons, bumper stickers, giveaways—the list was endless. They would set up interviews for the players at local radio and television stations. The budget ran into the millions.

To handle all this work, Samantha had to turn away numerous smaller jobs, some with clients that she hated to lose. In the past, those small jobs had been the company's bread and butter. The contract with the Rainiers would usurp all their resources. If Emerald succeeded, it would earn national exposure. Other corporate clients would notice the small company from Seattle and come courting. Samantha's fledgling firm would fly to a higher altitude in the ad business. With that flight would come money and prestige.

And if they failed? Samantha had not thought much about that possibility. Without consulting her accountant, she knew her business could not afford to lose. If Emerald failed to show Mr. Elliott a healthy return on all his advertising dollars, it would be stretched pretty thin, maybe too thin to recover. Nothing like putting all our eggs in one basket, Samantha had thought when she signed the contract.

"So, Bren, this is the big one. Let's get started. I want to schedule a kickoff meeting with everyone on Monday. Afternoon is best." She gathered up the photos.

Brenda jotted a few more notes on her pad of paper, then boosted herself out of the chair. "Right, boss. I'll set it up."

Samantha dropped the photos in the center of the mess on her desk. As if by magic, Jarrett's picture slid out of the pile. He smiled up at her.

"Wipe that cocky grin off your face, Jarrett Corliss," Samantha warned the man in the photo as she tapped his nose with the eraser end of her pencil. "I've got plans for you."

Chapter Three

"Okay, sports fans. Here's the pitch," Samantha announced.

Her staff groaned loudly, their heads falling limp to rest on the conference table in mock anguish.

Samantha grinned. "Yeah, yeah, yeah. Show some respect here. I'm the boss and if I want to play sportscaster, you all get to listen in rapt silence."

A loud, wet raspberry cut across the end of her sentence and she scowled at the culprit. She should have expected it—Brenda. "Quiet! No dissension in the ranks." She softened the stern warning with a smile. Then, before she lost control of the unruly bunch, she plunged ahead with the meeting.

"As you all know, I met with the Rainiers last week. Here's the schedule I've penciled out for what needs to be done." She passed a stack of papers around the table. "First, I have a meeting with Elliott and his people on Friday. We have to have presentation DVDs by then."

There were several moans of protest.

"I know. It's a push, but we need to roll in high gear. The photographer is scheduled to reshoot the team photos next Tuesday. The first commercial will be shot the middle of the following week, probably Wednesday and Thursday, depend-

ng on Dietrich's schedule. We'll use photos or pull stills from
the video for billboards."

Before she could continue, Lane interrupted. "Wait a minute,
chief. What happened to all the time we were supposed to have
to get ready for this project? We've known about it for a month."

"You're right. But contract negotiations were delayed, so
we're up against the wall. The team leaves for spring training
camp in three weeks. All this has to be done before they go."
Samantha knew what the next few weeks were going to be
like—an unbroken string of long days and longer nights. She
didn't like it any more than her team did, but it was essential
that they attack it with all their enthusiasm and momentum.

"Hey, after three weeks of twenty-seven-hour workdays,
things should settle down to a more reasonable pace," she
added with a smile.

She paused to survey the faces around her. They all looked
interested, eager and alert. A little apprehensive, too. No harm
in that. No one was surprised by the amount of work. No one
complained.

"The tight deadline will mean a lot of work, but we can do
it. Brenda has a list of all the details to be covered that we'll
go over at the end of the meeting. First, I want to start with
the overall thrust of the campaign."

Samantha outlined the information she had on the Rainiers,
their recent history, changes in staffing, their strengths and
weaknesses. If her staff hadn't all heard this somewhere else,
she wanted to be sure they did now. To design a good advertising campaign, Emerald Advertising needed to somehow
magically erase the past. She wasn't fooling anyone about
how hard that would be.

"Let's bounce some ideas around. Nothing is too far-
fetched or corny at this point. Brenda, got your crayon and
notepad warmed up?"

"Ready, coach. Let 'em fly. I'll catch 'em." Brenda's penci[l] was poised to write, but the room was silent.

"Come on," Samantha coaxed. "I can see those wheel[s] turning. Spit something out. Anything."

"Okay," Lane began cautiously. "What about bikinis?"

"What about them?"

"Well, sports and women in bikinis just go together like, like—"

"Like safe and sex," Pam finished. A burst of laughter followed.

"I'm all for bikinis," Carol chimed in. "But only if the players are wearing them." More laughter greeted this sally. Samantha joined in, then guided the conversation.

"Lane has a point. The commercials that have been used during most major sporting events have featured any number of bikinis and skimpy attire to promote everything *except* swimwear and clothes. But how do we use them? We're promoting a baseball team. Is that a different market than beer commercials target?"

Samantha sat back and let the others debate the issue. Ideas were tossed out randomly. Bikinis and beer led—by a very circuitous route—to nuclear reactors and life preservers. She let them mine the raw possibilities of each idea for a while then pushed them off in another direction. Brenda wrote furiously, so every speck and notion was documented for future reference. Ideas and patterns of ideas mentioned in this session might even prove useful later for a completely different product. Brenda was a storehouse of past brainstorming sessions, any of which she might mention without warning to send them off in a new direction.

The discussion returned to its start and an argument raged back and forth about the ethics of using bikinis to promote anything. The women opposed it, the men were for it, so long as good-looking female models wore them. Then Lane yelled something crazy about extraterrestrials and the brainstorming took a decidedly odd turn. Samantha laughed and broke into the ruckus.

"Okay, guys. That's a little bizarre, even for me. I know I said nothing was too far-fetched, but come on, aliens in bikinis kidnapping a baseball team?"

"Sure, it'd be great," Stuart said, adopting Lane's brain-child for the moment. "Like Willie Mays meets ET. But with less cellulite."

"Yeah. The players could be sucked up into this ship. Then weird creatures would operate on them and make them better players." Carol picked up Stuart's thought and gave it another twist.

When this craziness had run its course, Stuart asked the question Samantha had been waiting for. "What do *you* have in mind for this campaign, Samantha? We've been spilling our guts for over an hour, but you haven't offered much yourself."

"Well. I've heard some good ideas passed around today, except the one about aliens." She shook a finger at Lane. He smirked. "But I want to focus a little tighter on the problem before we look for solutions. The Rainiers are a bunch of druggies and bullies, and no one wants to go to their games because they always lose. Right?" There were nods of agreement.

"To change that perception, we need to recast the Rainiers as a completely new team. The old is gone. Here's this new gang of kids that no one knows anything about. It's our job to introduce them and show how they're starting out fresh." She paused for emphasis. "So I think we should show what the players were like in grade school."

"Grade school?" was the startled question from several people.

"Yep. Grade school." Samantha went on to outline her idea as she had to Brenda. "What if we set them up as a sandlot team on the playground. Make their individual talents come from something they did then. Exaggerate to show how they started out in the game."

This set everyone into another flurry. Ideas spun around the room like Frisbees.

"Like the kid that hits a home-run ball through the plate glass window two blocks away," Lane said.

"Or a pitcher that used to hit birds with rocks," Stuart added.

"No. That's too mean. Besides, the animal-rights activists would have a cow," Carol countered. "How about throwing newspapers on a paper route. Or winning all the Kewpie dolls at the county fair. Something like that."

"But what about the aliens?" Lane asked plaintively. Everyone laughed.

The group's creative juices flowed freely. Once a basic theme was set, their ideas began to mesh. At the end of the meeting Samantha knew they were on to something good. She divided her staff into two creative teams—Stuart and Lane in charge of one, Carol and Pam the other. Then she assigned several of the more urgent items on Brenda's list.

"Everyone know where we're going and what we're doing?"

There was a chorus of acknowledgment.

"Good. I want both groups to work closely with one another on this. It all has to mesh. Let's meet again on Wednesday afternoon to go over the preliminaries. If you have any questions, I plan to be in all week. Thanks, gang." The meeting was over.

Samantha watched as they exited en masse. Pam and Carol were already sketching ideas in the air for the project. Between them, she knew she'd have some good, solid stuff by midweek. Samantha crossed her fingers and hoped the Rainiers would be just as excited.

The wait to find out how the Rainiers felt didn't take long, or at least it seemed that way. The week flew by and before she knew it, she had delivered her pitch to Andrew Elliott and the rest of the Rainier managers and coaches.

"A skookum presentation! I like it." Elliott pounded his cigar into the ashtray on his desk. He was about sixty years old with the energy of a teenager. His short, round frame and rosy cheeks held all the good humor of Santa Claus. Except when he was crossed. Then he could outdo both Scrooge and the Grinch. The cherubic exterior hid a core of pure steel.

"Thank you, Mr. Elliott. If you're satisfied, we'll get the first commercial ready to shoot in about a week."

"It's wonderful, Ms. James. The campaign's shaping up to be a real corker. Just what this team needs."

Samantha chuckled at his quaint colloquialism. "I'll let your staff know where and when we begin shooting as soon as I make the final arrangements with the director and the camera people." She shook Elliott's soft, chubby hand. As gentle as his grasp felt, Samantha knew it cloaked the proverbial iron fist with which Elliott ruled his organization.

Before she won the contract with the Rainiers, Samantha had wondered why Elliott had let the organization run so far into the dirt. Fearlessly, she asked him that exact question early in their negotiations. She had a lot at stake by taking on a project this size. If the owner wasn't committed to bringing the team up to par with the rest of the league, there was no reason to stick her company's neck out. After all, the advertising contract only covered one season. If the team did well—that is, if the stands were full—it would be extended to the next season. The gamble was acceptable to Samantha only if Andrew Elliott had the wherewithal and desire to pull the team from the bottom of the standings. Otherwise, what was the point?

Her direct and candid question was one of the ways she had impressed Andrew Elliott. He admitted his mistake: turning too much power over to the wrong man. His confidence had been misplaced, and he had found out only after disaster struck. Consequently, ninety-nine percent of management had been fired—*canned* was his word. Now Elliott was making the decisions, and the team would change. Which was not saying it was a sure thing. If they didn't improve, Elliott planned to put the whole kit and caboodle on the auction block and sell to the highest bidder. Samantha liked his honesty, and despite the high stakes, she had signed the contract.

"I'll talk to you Monday morning. The team photos are scheduled for Tuesday. I left a copy of the details with your secretary."

Once out of the office, Samantha did a little dance of elation. The campaign was going exactly as she had hoped. Impulsively, she decided to walk over to the ballpark. Where better to revel in this small success? Besides, inspiration had hit her there before. Maybe another bolt of ideas would come with a new visit. She still had to catch up to Boomer, too.

Management offices for the Rainiers were in a four-story structure just north of the stadium. As she strode toward the main entrance, she was struck by how little Sicks Stadium looked like a ballpark. With its brick-and-wood facade, the old structure looked more like a large factory. Inside, a pitched roof covered the horseshoe-shaped stands. Like other stadiums built in the early part of the last century, the playing field was open to the elements.

She showed her badge to the security guard and wound through the maze of tunnels to the field, following a path she had memorized on her first visit. She didn't see anyone until she climbed out of the dugout onto the field: a few players and coaches stood near the bullpen. Samantha ignored them and slowly turned in a circle, taking in the entire spectacle.

Anticipation filled the air, as if the old building was waiting for the season to begin. After so many summers of baseball, so many games won and lost, maybe the fanciful sensation was true. Maybe this place, like the fans that would fill the seats, waited impatiently for winter to end and another long summer to begin. She laughed at herself: she had definitely been spending too much time thinking about baseball.

JARRETT PICKED UP A new ball, gripped it loosely and slowly pulled his arm back to throw. He went through a pantomime of a pitch in slow motion, not actually letting the ball leave his hand. He repeated the movement over and over, loosening his arm and shoulder muscles. As they warmed, he could feel them easing, a fluidness coming in where rigidity had previously lay. He exaggerated the motions of pitching to work his entire arm, up into his back, down to his legs and toes, preparing his body for the real thing, the whole business of muscle and bones working together in perfect harmony.

Or not.

Jarrett had once taken the gift of painless motion for granted. Not so long ago, those muscles worked perfectly, giving him the control to pitch a baseball however he chose, as fast as he chose. He could fine-tune each pitch to place it low or high, inside or out, with any sort of spin the catcher signaled. And speed? His fastball was a thing of glory. These days, he struggled to reach that perfect grace. When it did return, it was often accompanied by grinding pain.

Nor had he always been so aware of the muscles in his arm. He had known the names of the major muscle groups, but that was it. Now he knew, down to the tiniest connective tendon, the name and function of each part of his shoulder: deltoid, trapezius, teres minor, teres major, scapula. He swore he could feel each one during his slow warm-ups. Learning how his body worked had been one of the ways he had kept his sanity during the long recovery. He had thought that if he understood the anatomy, he could somehow heal faster. It *had* helped him focus during therapy. With every pinch of discomfort or stab of outright pain, Jarrett would name the muscle and think beyond the agony. He supposed his method had worked, since he was pitching a baseball again, but at a price. His shoulder never completely stopped hurting him and control was elusive.

"All right, Corliss," the pitching coach yelled from the other end of the bullpen. "Let's see some heat."

Jarrett stepped up to the mound and took his stance. He tried not to think about anything at all. *Just throw the ball.* The first pitch was wild, and Jarrett winced. The second wobbled a bit, but made the strike zone. With each throw, he tried to place the ball where he wanted it to go. Speed would come later in the session.

The coach stood, arms folded across his chest, hat pulled low over his eyes. Jarrett couldn't read his expression and hoped his own was as blank. Training was always this way, from bad to better with each pitch. He just wished he didn't start at square one each day.

"Try dropping your shoulder a bit on the follow-through," the coach said, coming toward Jarrett. He picked up a ball and mimed his request. "I think you're too high when the ball is here. See?"

Jarrett continued his practice, but control came hard. A few balls would be on the money, but the next would fly wildly astray. He felt frustration rise, which did nothing to help his game. He knew the coach was unhappy, too. As they discussed another tactic, Jarrett caught a flash of red out of the corner of his eye. When he looked, he was surprised to see Samantha James climb the steps out of the dugout and walk onto the field. The coach spoke again and Jarrett wrenched his attention back to his job, but his concentration was abruptly shattered. What was she doing here? And how could he get away from practice long enough to talk with her?

He had spent considerable time thinking about the lovely advertising executive. He hadn't had a chance to pursue his attraction to her, but here was his opportunity. If he could just get away for a moment. The coach tossed him a ball. Jarrett wound up and threw. Perfectly. He blinked.

"Hey! Whatever you did, do it again," the coach demanded.

Jarrett followed orders, and the pitch sailed over the plate. Without a word, the coach threw him more balls, and Jarrett pitched them. Each one flew as good as the first. Control was suddenly back in his hands.

The coach walked up to Jarrett. "What's the deal, Corliss? You been holding back all this time?"

"Not on purpose." Jarrett was as amazed as the coach. *Where had this control come from?* He looked over to be sure Samantha hadn't left yet and an idea occurred to him. "Maybe I've been using the wrong lucky charm," he said slowly.

The coach followed his gaze and saw Samantha. "Nice. And better looking than that mangy rabbit's foot Seibert wears around his neck. Is she yours?"

"No," Jarrett admitted, sharing a grin with the other man. "But if you give me a break, I'll make that a yes."

The coach chuckled. "Sure, Corliss. Go for it."

Jarrett pulled off his glove and opened the gate on the bullpen. As he jogged over to her, he remembered how hot her gaze had been, stroking along his skin. This time there would be no interruptions. There was no telling what progress he could make today. He was back in control.

THE SUN MAGICALLY APPEARED for a moment to brighten the
wet grass of the infield. Samantha took a deep breath of air
and smelled her past: early mornings spent at the ballpark with
her father and brother before school started, the air cool and
damp, the grass wet with dew. Here she was again, wondering why the game had fascinated so many for so long. And
how could *she* make one team recapture that allure and fill all
these seats? Was she the right person for the job? Too late for
second thoughts, she reminded herself.

"If you're looking for someone," a voice announced, "he's
right behind you."

Samantha spun to face the man she had consistently
banished from her thoughts over the past week. "Jarrett!" she
said. "I mean, Mr. Corliss."

"The first name suits me best." A slow, warm smile creased
his face. "It's right nice of you to come all the way over here
to check on me."

That smile, coupled with the gleam in his eyes, sent her
heart fluttering. The visceral attraction she had felt in the
locker room was back in full force. Samantha was breathless.
She struggled once more to pull a cloak of professionalism
over her jangled nerves. "I'm checking up on the *whole* team.
Not just you."

"Check up on me as much as you want, darlin'," he drawled,
a twinkle in his eyes. "You're great for my game. As soon as I
saw you standing over here, my pitches started smokin'."

"Oh, stop," Samantha said. "All this flattery makes my
heart go pitty-pat."

Jarrett laughed. "Can't be flattery if it's true."

Samantha rolled her eyes at that. "I just stopped by to
check on a couple of items for the ad campaign," she said
lightly. "We'll be shooting the commercials soon."

"On Tuesday?"

"No, that's a photo shoot for new close-ups and team shots, things like that." Samantha gave Jarrett a cool smile. "Well, it was nice to see you again, Mr. Corliss, but I have to get back to my office."

She turned away, looking for the nearest exit, anxious to put distance between her and this too compelling man. He stepped close and stopped her, encircling her wrist lightly with calloused fingers.

"Not so fast, we're just getting warmed up here."

"The inning is over, Mr. Corliss. It's time for you to go back to your dugout."

"Come on, Sammy, I haven't even had a chance to throw one yet. Have dinner with me tonight."

The question surprised her. The impulse to say yes surprised her even more. "Strike one, Mr. Corliss."

"Didn't I just put one right over the plate?"

"Sorry, no. That one was wild."

"Tomorrow night then."

"No. Thank you, Mr. Corliss, but no."

"Why not?"

She tugged away from him, but he only let her get half free. Her wrist slipped through his fingers until they were holding hands, then he tightened his grip. She eyed him warily. "What difference does it make? No is no. Let go of me, please."

Jarrett ignored her request and stepped closer to her. He ran a finger down her cheek and over her chin. The touch was so electric that Samantha's hand tightened around his, and the desire she could see so plainly in his eyes mesmerized her. She felt as warm as she had in the locker room, when he had been wearing only a damp towel. All her good intentions vanished. When he spoke, his voice was low, a thread of amusement running through the words.

"Well, sometimes 'no' is just 'maybe' wearin' a different dress. Come on, Sammy," he coaxed, threading his fingers through hers. "Have dinner with me tonight."

Samantha was struck by the look of complete and utter assurance on Jarrett's face. He was certain she would say yes, just because he wanted her to do so. He was just as cocky and arrogant as all the others. She tugged her hand back sharply, breaking the connection and stepping away.

"Well, in case you hadn't noticed, I'm wearing a business suit. When I say 'no,' I really do *mean* no."

"Give me a chance, Sammy. If we're going to be working closely together—"

"I assure you, we're not going to be spending that much time together, Mr. Corliss."

"Jarrett. Please." His eyes were an innocent blue, but the dimple in his cheek gave his teasing away. Samantha felt a smile tug at her lips. Really, he was too charming for his own good—or hers.

"Jarrett," she said reluctantly. "No matter what we call each other, my answer is still no. Besides, I don't date people I work with."

He frowned at that, all teasing gone from his face. "We aren't working together. I pitch baseballs, you pitch the team."

"That is working together," she insisted calmly. "At least we both work for the same man. And Andrew Elliott has definite ideas about how he wants the team run this year. One of them is that no one from my company gets personally involved with the team."

"I can't believe Elliott cares diddly about us having dinner."

"Trust me, he does. He wants business to stay business."

"It'll be our secret then."

"This conversation is ridiculous. It doesn't matter what Andrew Elliott thinks—even though I happen to agree with him. I said *no,* thank you. That's all I have to say." Exasperated by his stubborn arrogance, she turned and walked toward the stands.

Jarrett followed every step of the way. "Then what about you and Boomer?"

"Boomer?" She looked over at him, thrown off by the mention of her brother. "What does he have to do with this?"

"If you agree with Elliott, then what are you doing cozying up to Boomer? You two were pretty chummy in the locker room the other day."

Samantha tilted her head, looking up at him, confused by the direction the conversation had taken. What was he talking about? Then, in a flash, she realized. He thought she had a thing going with *Boomer.* The very idea made her want to laugh. "Boomer's different."

"I'll say. So what's Elliott think about you and him?" Jarrett said with a scowl. "If he gave his blessing to your seeing some second-rate left fielder, I don't see why he'd object to you having dinner with a starting pitcher."

"Boomer is *not* second-rate."

Jarrett snorted. "Okay, I'll take that back. He gets the job done. I just wouldn't trust guys like him."

"What do you mean, 'guys like him'?"

"Guys who think the rules are made for everyone else but them."

"That's who you think Boomer is?"

"I do."

Samantha folded her arms. "Why do you think that?"

He was silent.

"Come on, Jarrett," she prompted. "Out with it. What rules are we talking about? What rules has he broken?"

"Rules like corking your bat, gambling on the team, you name it, he'd do it."

"Has he actually done those things?"

"Not that I know about," Jarrett admitted. "Maybe he's done something worse that no one knows about. I wouldn't put it past him. Boomer's the kind of guy who's going to get caught someday doing something illegal and probably stupid. He's too arrogant."

Samantha would have laughed if she hadn't been so angry. Talk about the pot calling the kettle black. She shook her head. "I don't think you know him at all, Jarrett. I don't know how you could, you've only been on the team—"

"I don't need any time at all to know what Boomer is like. It's plain for anyone with half a brain to see." Jarrett threw his hands up in the air and stalked a short distance away before turning to face her again. "Come on, Samantha, he'd steal from his *grandmother* if it suited him, and he'd sleep like a baby at night afterward."

"He would not."

"Yeah, he would. He's got the least conscience of anyone I've ever met. You think you're special to him?" he asked with a sneer. "Don't bet on it. He's juggling more women than any man I've ever known."

"It's not like that—"

"No? So, it doesn't bother you to hear you're just one of the harem?"

"No. Even if it were true," Samantha said in a cold, furious voice. "Because if *you* had half a brain, you'd know that Boomer *James* is my brother."

With a contemptuous look, she turned her back on Jarrett and stalked away. Too angry to think, she stomped up the steps, through the tunnel, to the nearest exit. Just as she pushed the door open, Jarrett caught up to her and grabbed her by the arm.

"I'm sorry. I *am* an idiot. I didn't even know the guy had a last name."

"Most people do, Mr. *Corliss*." Samantha glared at him, then at the hand that restrained her. He dropped her arm.

"I'm sorry for what I said about Boomer. I thought—"

"Forget it."

"Please let me make it up to you, Samantha," Jarrett pleaded. "I'd really like to take you to dinner."

She laughed incredulously. "No thanks. I think we've spent enough time chatting."

"Please, Samantha."

She reined in her anger. "Look, Jarrett, you're entitled to your opinion about my brother. I think—I *know*—you're wrong, but I'm not going to argue about it. I accept your apology. Let's just leave it at that."

Their eyes warred for a moment. She could tell he wanted to keep arguing, but he held his tongue. Not too bright, but he was learning. He had dug himself a hole from which there was no easy way out. She pushed the door open and walked away without another word. This time, he didn't follow.

Back at Emerald Advertising, the expectant faces of her entire staff eagerly welcomed Samantha's return, like a nest full of baby birds waiting with hungry mouths wide open. She was still furious with Jarrett and would have preferred to fume privately in her office. But she couldn't let that anger spill over onto this moment. Her staff had worked too hard this past week and deserved a bit of jubilation.

"Well? How did it go?" Brenda demanded. "Did they like it?"

"It went fine," Samantha said as she set her briefcase down on a convenient desk.

"Fine? Fine!" Brenda screeched on behalf of the group. "What kind of answer is that?"

"Well, I suppose that it's a *fine* answer," Samantha responded flatly. "What do you want me to say? That Elliott loved the idea? That he practically did cartwheels over the presentation?" Her eyebrows were raised as she surveyed the tense group of people blocking the path to her office.

"Well, okay." She smiled broadly. "He practically did."

Her news took a moment to sink into their weary brains.

"He liked it?" Lane asked.

"*Really* liked it?" Carol added.

"Really, honestly and truly." Samantha's answer caused whoops of relief and shouts of happiness.

"Guys. Guys!" she yelled to get their attention. "Yes, he loved the entire concept. If he could do cartwheels, I think he would have. Now, we have the go-ahead for the first commercial and the photo shoot and that means lots of work. Take the rest of the afternoon off, but I need everyone here tomorrow morning. I promised three weeks of hell and we have two more to get through." As the gang turned to leave, she added, "We'll have a staff meeting first thing in the morning. Eight o'clock. Breakfast will be served."

She turned to Brenda, who still stood by her desk. "Brenda, we're on a roll. We're on a roll."

Chapter Four

Awash in tall, broad-shouldered men in various states of dress and undress, the studio was any woman's fantasy come true. The men stood or sat, singly and in groups, talking, bantering, laughing. All of them were muscular and attractive. When required, each one posed against the backdrop as instructed, flexed his muscles and hammed it up for the camera, strutting his stuff. Samantha dragged her attention away from the alluring sights and back to the photographer who was speaking to her.

"We're almost done with the portraits. I think we'll finish up before lunch. After that, I'll do the group shots. Sound good?"

"Fantastic, Carl," Samantha replied, looking down on the short photographer's balding head. "Whatever you need. I'll make sure everyone stays in line."

Since he was perhaps the best photographer in the city, Samantha had practically begged Carl to squeeze the Rainiers' shoot into his schedule. He was booked through August, and the prospect of national exposure meant little to his successful studio. To seal the deal, she had to promise him that she would redesign the brochure for his business, completely gratis. Costly for Emerald Advertising, but it would be worth it. Carl's work was impeccable.

Samantha turned her attention back to the players milling around her. Each one had a teasing remark or joke for her. Boomer kept demanding that he be shot on his "good side." Meeting each man individually in the locker room had been a stroke of genius. Now, everyone was relaxed and genial, anxious to look and act his best for her sake. The players leaped to follow her suggestions. She could ask each one to stand, sit or pose a particular way, and they did without a whine or a grimace.

Except for one. Jarrett had been quiet all morning. If he spoke, it hadn't been to her. Samantha was glad he kept his distance. What he had said about her brother still rankled. Today, she wanted nothing from the handsome pitcher but a few poses before the camera. The rest of the time, he could sit in the corner and sulk all he wanted.

Despite telling herself this, Samantha was all too aware of his every move. That bone-deep attraction she felt for him was still operating full force, alongside her anger. He didn't have to speak to get her attention. He only had to blink an eyelash, and she was on full alert. She kept her distance until she could avoid speaking to him no longer.

"Jarrett, Carl will need you in front of the camera next. If you'll follow me, the makeup people will get you ready."

Jarrett rose from his seat and walked to her side. His eyes locked on hers, sending a message that she didn't want to read. "Right this way." She gestured to the other side of the studio and turned her back on him.

Jarrett put a hand on her arm to slow her down. "I'm sorry about opening my big mouth Friday—"

"Really, Jarrett." Samantha did not slow her pace. "I accepted your apology. Let's just forget about it."

"You'll have dinner with me, then?"

These words made her stop in her tracks. "Let's not start this again. Not here."

"I'll buy you a drink."

"No."

"So, you haven't really forgiven me."

"This has nothing to do with what you said about Boomer. I told you Friday that I don't date people I work with and—" she held up a hand to stop his protest before he could voice it "—according to Andrew Elliott, we *do* work together. End of discussion."

"It doesn't say anything about you in my contract," he said stubbornly.

Samantha lowered her voice, conscious of the people all around them. "Jarrett, please listen to me. We can't have dinner, drinks or even milk and cookies. Mr. Elliott has given me explicit warning that no trace of scandal is to come anywhere near the Rainiers. If it does, and I'm responsible for it, my contract is kaput. And so is my business."

"One date does not constitute a scandal."

"What if someone sees us and decides it's news? It would be bad," she said, shaking her head. "Really bad. The vultures are circling, just looking for carrion to feed on again. If we're seen and the story gets in the paper, tongues will start to wag. People will wonder how I got the contract to promote the team. They'll put two and two together, come up with six and conclude that I slept my way into the job. Business as usual with the Rainiers. Worst of all, Elliott will hear about it and fire me."

"Samantha, I really don't think one date between us matters to anyone but you and me. Our private lives are our own, and what we do off hours is our own business. Not the sports editor's, not the coach's, not even Andrew Elliott's."

"If it were that simple, we wouldn't be having this conversation."

"You mean you'd have gone out with me the first time I asked you?"

"No. And I won't go out with you now." With that, she turned and walked briskly away. He could follow her or not, right now she didn't care. Once again, his arrogance rubbed her the wrong way. Why couldn't he see how much they risked even just talking about it here and now?

After a break for lunch, Samantha, Carl and his assistant gathered the players for group shots. The power hitters were grouped together, then outfielders, then infielders, for formal and informal poses. As Carl photographed the infielders, Samantha went around gathering the pitchers for their turn. Jarrett was sitting alone again, off to one side.

"Jarrett, Carl will be ready for you in about fifteen minutes. Could you please stand with the other pitchers over behind the lights? The cosmetician might want to touch up your face a little."

"I can't."

Samantha, who was already moving away to speak to another player, turned around. "What did you say?"

"I said, I can't."

She stared at him as if he had grown another head. His face was solemn, but the dimple beside his mouth twitched. "Please, Jarrett. Everyone else is ready."

He shook his head. "Sorry. I think I ate too much for lunch. My tummy hurts. I'd better go lie down."

She felt a brief surge of panic. "You can't lie down," she protested. "There's no time to reschedule this."

"Where's the little boys' room? I think I'm going to be sick." He let out a completely unconvincing moan.

He was faking, and not even doing a good job of it. He obviously wanted her to know that, too. "What are you up to?" she snapped.

"Up? Oh, don't say that word. It makes me queasy." He clutched at his stomach and moaned again, louder and more melodramatically this time. But the dimple was there, too, taunting her.

"Stop it, Jarrett."

"I can't help it if I don't feel good. Sorry. You'll have to take my picture some other day."

Samantha was furious. What did he think he was doing with this corny bit of playacting?

"Jarrett, please cooperate. Carl only has these last few shots to do and you're done for the day." She found herself pleading and hated herself for it. She had no choice.

Jarrett seemed to ponder her request. Slowly, he raised his eyes to hers. "I might be able to do it. If you'll help me."

"What do you want from me?"

His eyes locked onto hers. "Go to dinner with me tonight."

"What?" Samantha shouted.

"Shh!" Jarrett held a finger to his lips. "You're making a scene. We don't want to start a scandal, now, do we?" He grinned broadly, eyes dancing with laughter.

Samantha was livid. "The answer is still no, Mr. Corliss. It won't *ever* be yes." She whipped around to stalk off, but Jarrett stopped her once more.

"Owwww, the pain."

Samantha turned back to face him. "You can't do this!" She sucked in a breath and tried to calm down. When she spoke again, she held her voice even, without tempering her anger. "I have had enough of your games. Being in these shots is not a choice you can make. It's part of your contract."

"Not if I'm sick." Jarrett's answer—his calm intransigence—astounded Samantha. "Section eleven, I think, near the top of the page. It covers all kinds of injuries and ailments—headaches, backaches, hangnails, hangovers. You name some disease or complaint, it's probably in there. I believe tummy ache is specifically mentioned somewhere in the middle of the list."

"But you are *not* sick. You're faking it."

"Well, I *feel* sick. Maybe it was the food. Or maybe I'm lovesick. Maybe if I lie down for an hour."

Samantha counted to ten, then said through gritted teeth, "I have no more time to waste on you, Jarrett. Get in front of that camera, or I'm calling Mr. Elliott."

"Better call a doctor instead." His look radiated pure innocence. "I think I'm running a fever. Feel my forehead."

She wanted to grab him by the throat and throttle him. She continued, in as reasonable a tone as she could muster, "I can have your ass for this, you know."

Jarrett laughed. "Darlin', you can have any part of me you want." He sobered, his face becoming hard, his eyes drilling into hers. "Getting sick is not a breach of contract, Samantha. And if you think I'm malingering, just call the doctor. I'm sure after an afternoon of his poking and prodding, I'll feel better by tonight. But I'm equally certain if you say 'yes' I'll feel better in a jiffy." His voice was soft, his tone matter-of-fact, but his eyes told her he would not back down.

Samantha saw no way out, but she tried one last time to escape. "This is blackmail, Jarrett."

"Is it?" Jarrett asked, smiling agreeably. "Does that mean you'll go out with me?"

This was not the kind of attention she needed or wanted right now, yet she felt the blood sizzle in her veins. *He's crazy,* she thought. *And he really wants me.*

"My company is at stake here, Jarrett. My future." She hoped the appeal would work. It didn't.

"The only thing at stake is dinner, Sam. Steak or fish, chicken or vegetarian. Whatever you want to eat."

Samantha threw up her hands. "Fine. Pick me up at eight and keep this to yourself." She glared, pointing a finger at him. "If I hear or read one peep about this, this…date from anyone, you're dead."

"Okay. But let's make it seven o'clock." Jarrett stood, fully recovered, and walked with her to where the other pitchers were gathered. "I already made reservations."

Samantha's look of openmouthed astonishment set him laughing again. She wanted to slap him.

Carl called the pitchers to line up, and Jarrett strolled in front of the camera.

Brenda appeared at Samantha's side. "What was that all about?" she asked in a whisper. "It looked like you were going to kill him there for a second."

"I almost did," Samantha answered, her fists clenched in anger. She turned away to help Brenda line up the next group of players. "And I might yet."

SAMANTHA TOOK HER TIME showering, applying her makeup and changing her clothes. Dinner tonight was one date for which she would gladly be late. After the photo shoot, she had fled to her office and the phone messages littering her desk. Everyone had questions to be answered both in the office and out. Stuart and Lane had argued over the video mock-ups and had to be soothed. Brenda thought she was going into labor, but it turned out to be an overdose of chili peppers for lunch. Then Andrew Elliott had called. Samantha's nerves were stretched tight, knowing she was defying his stipulation by going out with Jarrett. He rang off cheerfully. Of course, he knew nothing about it, but her tension didn't ease.

When she arrived home, she fell facedown onto the sofa and lay there, trying not to think. The stillness was a blessing. Eventually, she had to get up and think about the upcoming evening. Her composure, if not restored, was at least shored up. After a few hours of distance from Jarrett, she was having trouble with her anger again. The problem was that she wasn't angry enough. His acting sick and his unstoppable persistence just to get a date with her was amusing. She no longer felt mad at him. Somehow *that* struck her as a problem.

At least half of her wanted to go on this date. That silly, sentimental-idiot side thought his ploy to win her consent was flattering. The sensible part of her said she was crazy to take a chance like this. She should call him and cancel. She had the pictures she needed and there was nothing he could do about it. She was not obligated to keep a promise made under duress to a blackmailer.

Samantha stood up, resolved. She walked to the phone, then passed by it on her way to her bedroom closet. She opened the door and surveyed the contents. A knit dress in a shade of pale peach looked right for some reason. It had a scooped neck banded in darker peach, long sleeves and the skirt stopped just above her knees. Comfortable and not too daring, the dress suited a variety of occasions. She left her hair down.

Why let Jarrett swindle her into this date? Well, she hadn't *let* him dupe her, she just hadn't had any choice at the time. She had a choice now, but canceling would be stooping to his level of trickery. She would stick by her bargain no matter how he had extorted it from her. Besides, this was a meal between friends. She would make that clear to him. She would go, enjoy some good food and pleasant conversation, share a bottle of wine, then say good-night. Forget that he was handsome and very sexy. Forget that he would use any wile he could to turn a friendly evening to something more. Just forget all that. She stood in front of the mirror and attached golden hoops to her ears as the mantel clock chimed seven.

Before the last note of the clock had stilled, the doorbell

rang. Samantha, wide-eyed, stared at herself in the mirror, trying not to see the sudden wash of anxiety that flooded her face. He was here.

Friends. That's all we are. Just friends. The words resonated through her mind like a mantra—one that sounded false to her ears.

Chapter Five

Jarrett pressed the doorbell a second time. Uncertain of his reception tonight—or if he would get any reception at all—he was on edge. After all, he had tricked Samantha into this date. Maybe she had calmed down, he thought. It could happen. Remembering her furious face, he had his doubts. She might not be home at all. In an attempt to deflect some of her anger, Jarrett had dressed carefully for the evening. Navy trousers and a white silk shirt were much more formal than his previous outfits. He had left his much-worn, much-loved leather jacket at home, too, opting for a bulky heather-tweed sweater for warmth against the chilly night air.

When Samantha opened the door, he held his breath. She was beautiful, more beautiful than he remembered, from the top of her burnished hair to the long length of her legs in silky hose. She wasn't smiling, but she wasn't wielding an ax, either. That was a good sign. Maybe his luck would hold. He held a froth of white freesias out to her, their scent filling the small vestibule. Would the flowers ward off any hostile greeting she had planned? She looked startled, then smiled and took his peace offering.

"Oh, how lovely! Thank you, Jarrett." He watched as she buried her nose in them, inhaling deeply. She looked up at him with enigmatic eyes. "You didn't have to bring these."

"I wanted to," he said with husky sincerity. "As a way of saying thank you for agreeing to dinner."

"You didn't leave me much choice, did you?" she said coolly. As he opened his mouth to defend himself, she stood back for him to enter the condo. "Come in. Let me put these in water, and I'll be ready to go."

He watched as she glided across the room. Watching Samantha walk away from him was getting to be a regular pastime these days. Tonight, he hoped to get her moving in the other direction. She returned this time with the flowers in a clear fluted vase and put them in the center of the table.

"Beautiful," she said.

"Yes," he agreed, looking at her instead of the flowers.

She ignored his compliment. "So, where are we going tonight?"

"To one of my favorite restaurants. I hope you like Italian." Jarrett escorted her to the door. "I stumbled on it when I was exploring the city one day."

Samantha pulled a long gray overcoat from the closet, and Jarrett held it for her as she slipped into it. Belting the waist, she turned to face him. "I love Italian. And I'm hungry. Let's go."

Jarrett was glad to follow. Staying too long in her apartment was a trial for him anyway. In such an intimate, cozy place, it took his every effort not to gather Samantha in his arms. Even as he had held her coat, he thought about where he would like to touch her, to kiss her. He would start with her neck and work his way down her smooth back…. He forced himself to stop that train of thought. Patience, he reminded himself. Tonight he was only taking her to dinner. This was his chance to make up for his blooper about her brother. He contented himself with holding her elbow as they walked to his car.

He opened the door of his dark blue convertible SAAB.

The top was up on account of the weather, but Jarrett thought how gorgeous her hair would be whipping in a warm summer breeze. He settled her into the leather seat before striding around to the driver's side. He started the car and pulled out onto the wet road. The usual Seattle rain drizzled down creating a cocoonlike feeling, wipers flipping soundlessly across the windshield in a hypnotic rhythm.

With the car in motion, they were silent. Jarrett was hesitant to speak and break the fragile mood between them. They traveled across the bridge that connected West Seattle to the rest of the city. As the wheels spun up to highway speed, Jarrett made a comment about the weather simply to break the silence. By the time they reached the Ravenna district, on a hillside overlooking the University of Washington and the lake, they were sharing opinions about architecture around the city. It was a safe subject that demanded nothing from either one. She pointed out the Smith Tower, where her business was. It was a quaint old building in the midst of taller, blander modern skyscrapers. It stood out in a crowd much like Samantha stood out—at least in his mind anyway.

After driving once around the block, Jarrett found a parking place. He opened Samantha's door and helped her out, keeping hold of her hand when she would have slipped it from his. He met her eyes, daring her to pull away, but she only smiled coolly and let him keep this slight hold on her. In one short block, they stood before the restaurant.

Saluté was a small Italian bistro filled with the strains of violins and the scent of oregano. Jarrett had been here many times and found the atmosphere welcoming, the food excellent. Too bad it was raining. When the weather was fine, the restaurant threw open the large front windows and sent mouth-watering odors of Italian food wafting through the neighborhood.

"Good choice," Samantha remarked.

Jarrett held the door open for her to precede him. "You've been here before?"

"Yes, once, last summer."

Inside, at the front, a large, ornate bar flowed along one side to serve the waiting customers. At the maitre d's podium, Jarrett was greeted with Italian gusto by a portly man with a lavish mustache. At the same time, two men at the bar called a greeting to him. Jarrett smiled at the strangers, no doubt sports fans who had seen his picture somewhere, and nodded in their direction, but turned immediately to the older man.

"Tony, this is Samantha. She loves Italian food, and I promised her the best in town."

"Samantha! *Bellissima!* I am delighted to make your acquaintance." Tony kissed her hand, staring at her admiringly. "She's a pretty one, Jarrett. You sure she's with you?" Tony eyed Jarrett, then turned to Samantha. "You can do better than this country boy," Tony confided with a nod, pointing a large thumb at Jarrett. "I got a son that you would love."

Samantha laughed. "I'm happy to meet you, too, Tony." She slid a glance at Jarrett. "So you've got a son. Is he as handsome as you?"

Tony burst into robust laughter. "Oh, she's a quick one, Jarrett." He pulled her away from Jarrett to tuck her hand into the crook of his arm and lead her past the other waiting customers—as if they had ceased to matter.

Jarrett followed. "Tony, I believe you are tryin' to steal my girl from me," he drawled, deliberately playing up his country twang.

"Well, of course I am. I got four sons. Each one needs a wife. How else do you expect me to get any grandchildren?" Tony stopped at a table tucked in the corner next to a window. He helped Samantha out of her coat and into a chair as Jarrett sat across from her. "Now. I'm not gonna give you any menus. You take my advice and let Joey handle everything. He knows what's best tonight. I promise he won't steer you wrong." As he spoke, a thinner, younger version of himself came over to the table.

"Pop, what'd I tell you? We don't make promises here. Just good food." Joey was handsome, with black hair and deep brown eyes. He slapped his father on the back affectionately. "Jarrett. Long time no see." He shook Jarrett's hand.

"Joey, I'd like you to meet Samantha."

Joey smiled and took Samantha's hand as well.

"Your dad was only promising that you'd choose a great dinner for us."

Tony broke in, putting an arm around his son's shoulders, and addressing Samantha. "This is the one I was telling you about. Isn't he great? And just between you and me, far better than some baseball player."

Samantha looked from Jarrett to Joey and back again, then shrugged. "I don't know, Tony. It's a hard choice. Ask me again after dinner."

Joey looked at his father questioningly as Tony and Jarrett laughed loudly.

"You enjoy your dinner. I'll come back and check on you later." With this, Tony returned to his post at the front of the restaurant, and Joey took over.

"So. You'll start with some antipasto." It was an order, not a question. "And I'll bring you a bottle of red wine that will make you believe you're in Italy stomping the grapes."

"Thanks, Joey. We're in your hands."

Joey nodded and left them. Jarrett leaned forward in his chair and smiled at Samantha. Their corner table was partially concealed by a post and a potted fig tree, quieter than most of the restaurant. The window was fogged from the heat of the room and wafts of steam rising from heaping plates of pasta. In the air was the tangy scent of tomatoes and garlic. It surrounded them and seemed to carry them together to a world far away from Seattle.

"Well, what do you think so far?"

"It's wonderful. Last time I came was nothing like tonight." She paused, a quizzical smile on her lips. "You seem like one of their family."

"I practically am, I come here so often," Jarrett said with a laugh. "I started chatting with Tony the first night I came. When he found out I was a newcomer to Seattle he adopted me on the spot. His whole family works here." Jarrett smiled, remembering the warmth and welcome he had felt. "I come over whenever I'm in town."

"A few other people seem to know you, too."

Jarrett shrugged. "It's part of the job."

Samantha smiled. "Well, get ready for more of the same. At least *I'm* going to make sure that you and the team become famous."

Jarrett felt a twinge of annoyance. Enthusiastic fans did come with the job, but signing autographs wasn't his favorite task.

Joey arrived with their appetizer and a bottle of wine, a dry and pungent Valpolicella—perfect with the antipasto.

"See? What'd I tell you," Joey said. He left briefly and returned with a basket of coarse, Tuscan-style bread and told them what they would be having for the main course: linguine in a light tomato sauce loaded with shrimp, clams and scallops.

"You'll love it. Guaranteed," Joey promised. "It's a recipe from my grandmother—God rest her soul—when she was still in the old country. Plus, everything in it is fresh today." Joey left for the kitchen without waiting for their approval.

As they nibbled on bread and antipasto, Jarrett talked about the photo shoot. "You really knew what you were doing today. I was impressed. It's not easy to control a pack of wolves like that."

"It did go pretty well. Except for one particular rogue wolf."

Jarrett smiled, unperturbed. "You managed. I guess advertising must be a tough field, too."

Samantha nodded. "Lots of big dogs chasing little bones."

"Why did you decide to go it alone?"

"Well, basically I think my ideas are better than anyone else's," she answered.

Jarrett was startled by her frank boast, then chuckled when he saw the teasing light in her eyes. "Not afraid of tooting your own horn, are you?"

"Nope. If I don't, who will?" She took a sip of wine. "Advertising is not a job for the faint of ego," she added. "I worked for one of the big advertising firms here in town for a couple of years, but I wasn't getting anywhere. I couldn't get my bosses to take any of my ideas seriously because they were too different."

"But that's what advertising is all about, isn't it?" Jarrett asked with a frown. "Different ideas?"

"You'd think," she agreed. "But you'd be surprised how cautious people in the business are. They want what they know. If a particular campaign worked for one product, it must work for all of them. Unless someone shows them how a new idea could be even better, they stick with the same old thing."

"And you decided to be that someone."

"It was either that or claw my way up the corporate ladder in a big firm." She smiled softly, her eyes on some distant memory. "I didn't want to wait that long. So I printed up some business cards and started at the top of my own little mound."

"Sounds easy."

"It wasn't." She shrugged. "But if it was easy, where would the fun be?"

"So what's it like at the top?"

"Not so glamorous. At least I'm my own boss. I make my own decisions about what works and doesn't work for a product. I can hire the people I want to work with, pass on the clients I don't care for. Come to think of it, I'm the best boss I ever had."

Jarrett laughed. "I'll bet you're a damn fine boss. A damn good businesswoman, too, by the sounds of it."

Samantha paused, seriously considering his remark. "I've tried hard to make Emerald a forward-thinking company. I don't want to stagnate, to slip into how so many of my competitors operate. Every project should be new and different. Fresh. That's the hard part, staying fresh I mean."

"And you've succeeded?"

"We're getting there. We've won a couple of awards for ads that we've done. The Rainiers will be our first campaign with so much national exposure. We'll see how it goes."

Jarrett realized that not only had they both found their dream early in life, they had one more thing in common: the determination to make that dream happen. She set goals and reached for them with all she had. No excuses, no arguments, just plain old hard work to get what she wanted. He felt the same about his pitching. And, he also realized, the more he found out about Samantha, the deeper his attraction to her became. Before he could express his admiration, Joey appeared with two heaping plates of food.

"Presto!" he declared as he placed the dishes in front of them. "Enjoy." He picked up the bottle to fill their glasses with more wine. "Can I get you anything else?"

"No thanks, Joey. This should last me a few days," Jarrett joked and looked over to Samantha to see that she had all she needed.

"I'm fine for now, too, Joey. It looks superb. Thanks."

Samantha watched the waiter vanish into the kitchen, then turned to Jarrett. She had a soft gleam in her eyes that he couldn't quite interpret. "Not bad for a meal I was blackmailed into eating."

Jarrett was not about to offer apologies. "You can call it blackmail if you want." He toasted her with his wine. "I call it working the angles."

Samantha's eyes were focused on her meal, but she didn't let the subject go. "This really could cause problems, though. Mr. Elliott doesn't want anything to go wrong this season. If it does, he's selling the team."

"They didn't say much during contract negotiations with me, but I'd heard that this was make or break for the Rainiers."

"It doesn't bother you to put your career on the line here?" Samantha asked with evident surprise. "Isn't that a little sleazy of them not to be straight with you?"

It was Jarrett's turn to show surprise. "Samantha, my career is already on the line. If I don't do well this season, that's it, I'm gone. I had a shoulder injury, then surgery on my rotator cuff. It's healing, but if I don't have a hell of a season, it'll be my *last* season."

"Oh, I didn't know," she said, half apologetically, half sympathetically. She stopped eating. "It's just—" She paused, as if searching for words. "I've seen you on tape and I...well, I guess I just assumed you were the ringer Elliott had brought in to save the team."

Bitterness rose like gall. "Yeah, that's me, the ringer." Jarrett sat back and took a deep breath, fighting back his useless rancor. "I took this job because it was the only one anybody offered me." He smiled at Samantha. "So, you see, having people talk because we're on a date is the least of my worries."

Jarrett returned to his meal. Samantha was silent, staring at him intently.

"You seem surprised at what I said," he offered eventually.

"I am. You seem so cool about your possible demise."

"I'm not cool at all," Jarrett said. "I'm just a realist. I know I'm on the edge. That's a fact I won't deny. I can't deny it. But if I worry about that, then I turn my concentration away from my job—throwing a baseball. And if I lose concentration, I risk injuring myself worse than I already have."

He shifted his gaze to his plate, then back to her, feeling a little uncomfortable talking so much about himself. Her eyes were deep green, giving no hint of her thoughts. He struggled that much harder to make her understand.

"Until I was injured, I didn't think I would survive without pitching, standing on that mound, watching the catcher's signals, throwing the ball into the strike zone. It's so much a part of me that I couldn't see myself doing anything else— being anything else—but a ballplayer. But I lost all that, at least for a while. A couple of doctors said I would never pitch again. I was shattered, but I survived. I found other things to do with my time, things I enjoyed almost as much. That cured me of myopia. Now I know there's more to life than baseball and the mound. I still want to pitch, of course—especially now that I've recovered—but there should be something more important to win from life than a low earned run average or a twenty-win season. Dinner with you is one of those things."

Samantha looked startled. "I am not something to win, Jarrett."

"Wanna bet?"

Joey roamed back to their table and encouraged them to eat more, showing them a tray laden with pastry.

"You clean your plate, you can have one of these," he tempted, then glided off to another table.

Once he was gone, Jarrett smoothly shifted the tenor of their conversation to less serious subjects. He had made his point. Samantha was smart. She understood his determination to explore this electricity between them. As they ate their way through the pasta and into dessert, Jarrett also avoided any more talk about pitching or advertising or the Rainiers. Instead, they covered any and all other subjects that came to mind, from the environment, to politics, to the world scene. When coffee arrived with after-dinner drinks, they were both at ease with one another.

Samantha leaned sideways as though she were going to fall out of her chair. "I ate too much. I'll have to waddle out of here."

"I'll bet you have a cute waddle," Jarrett teased, leaning toward her, elbows on the table.

Samantha smiled but didn't respond. Her eyes were lowered as she toyed with her coffee cup. Jarrett reached across the table and touched her fingers, lacing his through them.

"Thank you." He kept his voice soft and intimate.

Her eyes flew to his. "For what?"

"For coming out with me tonight. You could have canceled after the photographer took my pictures."

He saw in her eyes that she had considered doing just that. Something had stopped her. She shrugged. "A deal is a deal. Even if I was tricked."

"Persuaded."

"*Tricked*. But I won't be again," she warned. The threat carried no heat, but she slipped her fingers away from his.

"But you might be persuaded? To have dinner again?"

Samantha laughed and shook her head. Joey came around with more coffee, and the moment was lost. Declining a refill, Jarrett paid the bill. They rose and walked to the door. Tony once more tried to get Samantha to reconsider his proposal on behalf of his son.

"Well, if you don't like Joey, I've got three others you could take a look at," he said seriously.

"Sorry, Tony," Jarrett cut in, sliding an arm around Samantha's waist and pulling her close to his side. "Even if she was interested, I'm not. Go steal someone else's girl."

Tony laughed loudly and bowed them out the door. Jarrett kept his arm around Samantha as they walked to the car, matching his stride to hers. They fit nicely together, her head just grazing his jaw. Her scent overwhelmed his senses. It was pure luxury to be this close to her. When he handed her into the car and had to separate from her, he felt the loss. They drove home in silence, each lost in their own thoughts. At Samantha's front door, she turned to bid him good-night.

"Thank you, Jarrett. I had a very nice time."

"I did, too."

Before she could open the door and end their evening, Jarrett reached out and ran a finger down her cheek to her chin, much as he had on Friday. Instead of stopping there, he exerted a light pressure and raised her face to his. He bent his head and slowly, gently, kissed her. The taste left him wanting so much more. Once, twice, he brushed her mouth with his. Her lips parted and he pressed a third kiss to them, this one deeper and longer. When her hands came up to rest against his chest, Jarrett's hands clasped her waist.

More than anything, he wanted to slide his arms around her and pull her close. He held himself in tight check. Her aroma tantalized. *Her bedroom—her sheets—would smell like this,* he thought. Sweet perfume and woman wrapped tightly together. It would be a scent to drown in. The kiss deepened as he slid his tongue into her mouth. She met his foray with teasing flicks of her own, sending his senses reeling. Jarrett's heart pumped, and his breathing grew ragged.

Before desire could overcome him, he lifted his head. He had to be patient. Samantha was wrong: she *was* a woman to win. But not in one encounter.

"Tomorrow night?" he suggested. "Just you and me?"

Samantha swallowed. Her tongue came out to wet her lips, and Jarrett nearly groaned aloud. She was making him want to chuck all his good intentions and patience.

"Jarrett, I just don't know. I did have a nice time, but seeing each other complicates my business with the Rainiers."

"Samantha—"

"No." She put a hand over his lips. "I don't *know*, Jarrett. Not yet. I need time to think. That's fair."

"Yes," he agreed reluctantly. "Fair, but not easy."

She whispered good-night and left him standing under the porch light. He hadn't gotten her to agree to see him again, but she didn't say no. She was as attracted to him as he was to her. He walked to his car, whistling softly under his breath. She was as good as his.

Chapter Six

"Okay. Whatever it takes. Just get it fixed and get rolling."

"Can you get rid of the feedback in the boom mike, John? I'm hearing a load of garbage down here."

"Move that over there. No. Over there!"

If the photo shoot had been chaotic, the set for the commercial was mass hysteria. Bodies in identical black caps and T-shirts rushed back and forth shouting instructions, questions, threats. Cameras, lights and microphones were cast around in a pattern understood only by the workers. The players from the Rainiers were shuffled around, too—just more pieces of gear to position on the set. The difference was the amount of grumbling.

Excitement had worn off quickly for the players. Instead of the glamour they had expected, the day on the set had been downright dull. There were no personal assistants to fuss over each player, no chairs with individual names stenciled on the back. The director rarely spoke to them. More often, his assistant or another production person pushed them into and out of their places. They had expected that filming the commercial was going to be an exciting, action-filled adventure—a minimovie with each one a Hollywood star. In truth, it was long, tedious and boring. A process that they, as actors, had little to do with until it came time for them to stand before the camera and say a few lines.

Samantha ignored them. The best she could do was keep her end of the production moving so that they could all get out of here soon with the best footage possible. She listened to Dietrich, the director, as he spoke, agreeing or disagreeing, even arguing when necessary. Anything to get the filming started. Finally, he stalked off to thrash someone else, and Samantha went on to consult with one of the camerawomen. Out of the corner of her eye she caught Jarrett staring at her. His gaze was as tangible as a touch, probably because he was angry with her.

She had dodged him for the past week, ever since their dinner date. She had not returned his phone calls, not acknowledged the flowers he sent to her office. Now she could evade him no longer. Here in the studio, he was constantly in sight, a reminder of the decision she had yet to make. Or, rather, the decision she had yet to tell him she had made. Why was she stalling? She knew he would be angry with her, but that did not entirely explain her procrastination.

She glanced over when his head turned away. Broad, muscular shoulders, bared in the overalls he wore for the commercial, gorgeous profile, dimple that flashed when he laughed at something another player said—the list of reasons to delay was endless. The list of reasons to move forward was not quite as long, but no less compelling.

She had to end it, once and forever. Now. Avoiding Jarrett was a mistake. Look where it had gotten her the last time: she was tricked into a dinner date. Worse, Jarrett's stunt at the photo shoot to get that date had drawn dangerous attention to both of them. Later, their conversation at dinner had shown her that Jarrett thought her fears ridiculous. He refused to believe a relationship between them carried any serious risk.

His disbelief had her questioning herself again. Was she really overreacting? To test this possibility, Samantha brought the subject up in a meeting with Andrew Elliott.

"What if one of your players became involved with one of my staff members?" she had asked, keeping her tone mildly curious and matter-of-fact.

Elliott looked across at her, eyes narrowed and hard. "Who is it? I'll string him up by his jockstrap."

Samantha somehow summoned a light laugh. "No one. It's just a hypothetical question."

Elliott frowned at her. "This is no laughing matter, Ms. James. If there is any fraternization, I want to know about it so we can nip it in the bud immediately. I won't tolerate even the *whiff* of anything that will put this team back in the headlines for anything but winning games."

"Nothing has happened," Samantha said, backpedaling hastily. "I was just recalling the conversation we had earlier about—"

"I can't stop you or anyone else from getting involved with one of the players, Ms. James," Andrew Elliott interrupted, his tone steely. "But I can tell you that I will be extremely— *extremely*—unhappy with you if it does happen and nothing gets done about it. I would be forced to take painful measures to counteract any bad publicity."

"Mr. Elliott, nothing has or will happen."

"Good. Let's keep it that way."

Samantha kicked herself for trying to be coy with such a shrewd player as Elliott. His pointed questions and threats had killed whatever hopes she harbored about her and Jarrett. So long as she wanted to work for the Rainiers, she could have nothing to do with the team's starting pitcher.

Besides the risk to her business, Jarrett was, after all, a baseball player. While she liked the sport—and was in the

middle of advertising a baseball team—a life dominated by
it was far from her ideal. Growing up with a brother who was
so dedicated to batting practice and Little League, she had experienced firsthand the egos and attitudes that accompanied
the game. It had consumed her and her whole family. She
doubted that Jarrett, and life with him, would be much different. At times, he had enough arrogance and ego to compete
with the best of them, even Boomer.

Finally, and not the least important, Samantha had a hard
time viewing Jarrett dispassionately when it came to the
campaign. His photos from last week's shoot were great—
even better than great. All Jarrett's sex appeal shone brightly
on eight-by-ten glossies. That was where the problem lay:
Samantha was beginning to want that sex appeal all for herself.

If she used his photos as the campaign required, Jarrett
Corliss was going to be a star. That was exactly what she had
intended from the start and exactly what the team needed.
Still, deep inside, she wanted to forget he was part of the team.
The idea that other women might see the photos, see the same
thing that she saw, and pursue Jarrett made her uncomfortable,
even anxious.

The conversation she had had with Brenda about baseball
players and mitt-muffins had come back to her again and
again. She had lost before when she came up against such
willing women. She knew she would be devastated if Jarrett
succumbed to the same offerings. And the mitt-muffins were
just the tip of the iceberg. If Jarrett became as famous as she
expected, he would have his pick of a myriad of women. She
felt a huge temptation to shuffle his photo to the bottom of
the pile, a sure sign she was losing her objectivity. He was a
commodity, and she was the vendor. She could not afford to
forget that.

Samantha sighed. She would tell Jarrett about her decision,

about how things stood between them, and soon. But she could at least wait until there were fewer people around. She turned, heading from one task to another, and ran in to Boomer.

"Hey, Sammy. How's it goin'?"

"Fine, Boomer. You like strutting your stuff for the cameras?" Samantha smiled at his grimace. "Pretty exciting, huh?"

Boomer whooshed out a breath. "Man, I've had more fun watching paint dry. What's with this deal? All these people running around, but nothing happening. When do I get to stand in front of the camera? I ain't getting any prettier, you know."

Samantha laughed. "Well, there were a few glitches this morning. Typical stuff. Things should move along like lightning from now on."

"Finally."

"What'd you expect, hotshot? This isn't the *movies,* you know," she teased.

He grew serious and tugged her arm. "Listen, do you have a minute? I've got something I need to ask you. Privately."

"Oh, Boomer, I'm swamped here. I'll catch you later, okay?"

"I really need to talk to you now, Sam," Boomer insisted. "Please."

Samantha frowned. "This really isn't the best time. Besides, I wouldn't exactly call this private," she said, glancing around at the chaos.

"We can go over there behind that big poster. It'll only take a minute."

Before she could protest again, her brother took her arm and led her over to the "poster" he had pointed out, a large backdrop of screaming fans. Samantha was annoyed, but she went along.

"Five minutes, Ray, that's all I can give you." She used her brother's given name to let him know he had irritated her. "Is this what you wanted to talk to me about the last week? I looked for you when I was finished with Coach Cummings, but you'd already left the stadium."

Her brother heaved a huge sigh. "Yeah, sorry about that. I thought I got it all worked out and I wouldn't have to bug you."

"What's wrong?"

"Well, I hate to ask this—I really *was* trying to do this without anyone's help—but I need to borrow some money."

"What for?"

"I've got a—a...cash flow problem with an investment."

"What exactly does that mean?" Samantha asked, alarmed.

"Well, I've got most of my cash tied up in a real estate deal and I need something to tide me over. The deal's solid. Really. I just need some time to make it work. You'd get the money back, I promise."

"Well, give me the details, Ray. What kind of real estate deal? It doesn't sound too solid if it's draining your bank account."

"I'm in with a group of investors doing a big development out on the Sammamish plateau. A shopping center. But one of the investors died. He didn't have a will, so we've got to wait for his estate to clear probate before we can go any further." He held up his hand, stopping her question before she asked it. "It's definitely going to work out, but, like I said, all my cash is tied up for a while."

Samantha considered the information. "How much do you need?"

"Ten thousand dollars."

"Ten thousand! That's not petty cash, Ray. Why so much?"

"I've got bills, Sam. Plus the investment needs funds in the front end to get things moving. I know it's a lot, but I'll pay you back. With interest even."

Samantha bit her lip. Ten thousand dollars was a lot of money, especially when so much of what she had was tied up right now. "What are your partners doing about this?"

"They're putting up their fair stake. I have to hold up my end of the deal, too." He paused and took her hands. "Please, Sammy. I need your help."

She was torn. As fiercely as she had defended him to Jarrett, she knew her brother well. He wasn't a cheat, but he *did* like to bend the rules. Boomer's schemes were legend in their family. He always had some plan to make the world a better place while coincidently making himself a pile of money. Why he wasn't satisfied with being an incredible slugger, she would never understand.

As aggravated as she could get with him, she and Boomer were still close. They always had been. Maybe this time he really had a good deal going. Building shopping centers sounded a lot more sensible than most of his schemes. If she helped him, under strict rules, maybe he would come through. The sister in her had to hope so.

"Okay, Ray," she sighed, looking at her watch. This time-out was costing her. "I'll lend you the money, but we'll have to work out the details later. I've got work to do."

Boomer grabbed her in a hug that lifted her off her feet.

"Wait a minute, wait a minute!" she said, pushing at him. He set her on her feet, and she pointed a stern finger at him. "I want your word that this is a *loan,* Ray, not a gift. In writing, too. And you have to pay it back within six months." She fixed him with a steady gaze. "Got it, hotshot?"

"You bet," he crowed. "Thank you, thank you." He hugged her again and this time she let him. Samantha couldn't help but smile at his infectious happiness as he swung her around.

"Okay! Okay! Put me down. I have *work* to do."

"Anything you want, Sammy," Boomer answered, setting her down. He brushed a finger over her chin. "I don't know what I'd do without you."

Samantha poked him in the ribs. "It's a good thing you won't ever have to find out."

Boomer pinched her chin, laughed and walked off to join his teammates. Samantha shook her head affectionately, following behind her brother. Just before she moved from behind the backdrop, Jarrett stepped around the other end. Samantha stiffened. Her time had just run out.

JARRETT GRITTED HIS TEETH when he saw Samantha tense. She *had* been avoiding him. He had wondered. It was so chaotic in the studio, he hadn't been sure if she was dodging him or simply busy. All morning he had watched her dart from person to person, task to task, in endless motion. She had spent little time with anyone but the director, so he could fool himself into thinking she was just doing her job. He had held his patience, even when he was told to change into the ridiculous overalls he wore. They made him look like a hillbilly. Boomer and Alvendia had been cracking jokes at his expense ever since he walked out of the changing room.

Samantha had told him she needed time to think, so he had backed off. As the days passed, he kept expecting to hear from her. The kiss they had shared still sizzled in his blood. It must have seared her, too. A few days after their date, Jarrett sent flowers to show her he was thinking of her. When there was no response, his frustration rose. Finally, he called her office, but was stonewalled by her secretary. He told himself that she was busy and held on to his patience by the thinnest thread.

Seeing her now, Jarrett knew before she spoke what her answer would be. "We need to talk."

"Not here."

"Yes, *here,*" he insisted. "You won't call me or see me anywhere but on the job. I am not waiting any longer."

Samantha bit her lip. "I'm sorry, Jarrett. I know I should

have called you, but I didn't know what to say. Actually, I know what to say," she continued before he could speak. "I just know you aren't going to like it."

"Our dating is not going to cause a scandal," he said flatly.

"Jarrett, we've been through this before." Her voice was tinged with exasperation. "My answer is no."

"Because Elliott will cancel your contract."

"Because I've had it up to *here* with jocks," Samantha said, slashing a hand across her neck. "What is it about you guys? Isn't the word *no* in your vocabulary? First Boomer and now you." She glared at him, eyes frosty. "Excuse me, I have a job to do."

Her attitude fired his temper. "Don't lump me in the same category as your brother. If you're so worried about scandal, what about *him?*"

"What are—"

"Why did you say yes to him, Sam?" Jarrett interrupted. "If anyone's headed for disaster, it's Boomer."

"What's that supposed to mean?"

"Come on, Sam," Jarrett scoffed. "You defend him, but you know as well as I do that he's an accident just waiting to happen. You're lending him money for some slimy real estate scheme. That's the sort of scandal that will send Elliott through the roof."

"That was a *private* conversation."

"Then you shouldn't have had it here."

"You're right. I shouldn't discuss personal matters on the job, where any *eavesdropper* can overhear." Samantha spoke through her teeth, arms crossed tightly over her chest, then turned on her heel and stalked away from him. Just before she stepped around the backdrop, she turned. "Don't even think of acting sick to get out of the commercial. I'll call Elliott, and in two seconds he'll string you up himself."

It was all Jarrett could do to keep from chasing after her.

He still had a few choice words to share with that woman. He strode back into the main part of the studio just as the assistant director called his name. He posed as instructed under the blazing lights, his mind far from the crew, cameras and cables swirling around him.

A woman in horn-rimmed glasses darted out and blotted his face with a towel while another patted his cheeks with a puff coated with some powder. The powder got up his nose and Jarrett sneezed, sending them scurrying. Seconds later they were back blotting and patting. He stood where he was told, spoke his few words twice, then a third time, and it was over.

As Jarrett stepped out of the artificial summer created by the lights, José Alvendia called to him. "Hey, *amigo,* you want a ride back to the park?"

"Yeah, just give me a minute to change."

Alvendia waved in assent, and Jarrett made his way to the dressing room and the first sink he could find. He had to get this itchy powder off his skin. He changed back to jeans and sweatshirt and grabbed his jacket. He considered confronting Samantha again, but decided it was better to wait until he could get her alone. What he had to say to her was not for public consumption. Jarrett hurried out to join Alvendia and Hank Wilson, the shortstop.

"That was the most boring day I've ever spent for thirty seconds sweating under those lights," Wilson complained.

Alvendia shook his head and laughed.

"Seemed like a goofy deal to me, man," Wilson continued as the men walked out the door and into the parking lot. "How are they gonna make a commercial out of that little bit of action? Nobody's gonna wanna see that."

"That's show biz."

They piled into Alvendia's car and headed towards Sicks Stadium through rain-soaked streets. At the stadium, Jarrett changed into his practice uniform and headed out to the bullpen. He needed to work off some steam before he confronted Samantha. What would he say to her? What would he do? She was right about one thing: he sure as hell wasn't taking no for an answer. That was certain. He blew out a breath and picked up the first ball.

All through his practice, the slow warm-up, his fastball, his slider, his curveball, Samantha was there. She had rattled him, but good. Her smile, her laugh and her taste filled his head. Strangely, it was no distraction to his throwing. Rather, it helped him focus—or unfocus—so that each pitch came naturally, without thought. Like that day in the park when he had pitched so well because she was there. Gradually, the desire and anger tangled up inside him was released.

From the bullpen, Jarrett went to the whirlpool and then to the showers. As the hot water beat down, he plotted strategy. Samantha would be completely wrapped up in the commercial for the rest of the day. He bet she would work long into the night. He would track her down tomorrow, at her office. He dressed and drove home, holding on to the calm that had enveloped him during practice. After today, the waiting was over. Time to play some hardball.

SAMANTHA STOOD, HAND TO her chin, wondering where the devil she could have put the proofs. She felt tired from yesterday's long work. She had not slept well, either, mostly addled by thoughts of Jarrett. Her desk, piled with paper, files on top of files, annoyed her this morning. Her worktable was inches deep in a similar mess and that annoyed her, too. Someday she would have to let Brenda clean up as she kept asking to do. Maybe the proofs got stuck in with the notes for her meeting.

"Samantha?" Brenda asked from the office doorway.

Samantha didn't look up from rummaging through the scattered piles on her desk.

"Bren, have you seen Lane this morning? He was supposed to have the final artwork for the Rainiers logo on my desk."

"Samantha, there's—"

"I've got an appointment with Elliott at two-thirty. We have to have it ready for his approval. It needs to go to the printers and uniform shop as soon as possible." She shifted one pile to the right. *Where were they?*

"I know, but—"

"Find him for me, will you? He's probably working with Stuart on the copy for the print ads. Now where are those proofs? They have to be here somewhere."

"Lose something?" a deep masculine voice asked.

Samantha's attention snapped up. Jarrett stood behind Brenda, towering over her. Her fist closed convulsively on the sheet of notepaper she held, crushing it into a ball. She felt a flush cross her cheeks and damned Jarrett for catching her so unaware. *Gorgeous,* she thought. How could the man look so good in jeans and a leather jacket?

"Mr. Corliss came to see you." Brenda looked up at Jarrett with a smile that bordered on adoration, and she looked as dazed as Samantha felt.

"Thanks, Brenda."

Brenda remained standing in the doorway.

"Don't you have something else to do?" Samantha prompted.

"Not really," Brenda said. "It's my lunch break."

Samantha's scowl did not dampen Brenda's smile, so she turned to Jarrett. "Well, Jarrett, this is a surprise. What can I do for you?"

She felt the tension in her body. The paper was still balled up tightly in her hand. Gorgeous or not, he was here to make trouble, especially after yesterday. She made an effort to relax, smoothing the paper she had crushed.

To her surprise, he held out a bouquet of flowers. Pink, blue, yellow and red, they were a treat to the eye on a dreary, rainy day.

"I came to take you to lunch."

Samantha looked at the bouquet, then at him. Slowly, she took the flowers, their delicate scents teasing her nose.

"Thank you, Jarrett. They're lovely." She looked down at his gift to avoid his eyes. "I'm afraid lunch is out of the question."

"Why not?"

"For one, I've got another appointment."

"Oh, I forgot," Brenda broke in. "George called a few minutes ago and canceled your lunch meeting."

Samantha glared at Brenda, who smiled back innocently. Jarrett looked between the two women. His face remained impassive, but the dimple in his cheek winked his amusement.

"Lucky for me, your schedule just cleared, Sammy. Come on. I'm hungry."

Samantha bared her teeth in a smile that was very close to a snarl. "We've said all we need to say to each other, Jarrett."

"Actually, we haven't," he countered evenly. "At least, I haven't."

Before she could argue, Lane appeared in the doorway, just behind Brenda. "You wanted to see me, boss-lady?"

Lane looked at Jarrett, obviously recognizing him from his photos and curious about why he was in Samantha's office. Jarrett remained silent, his hands in his jacket pockets.

"Yes, I did." Samantha gritted her teeth. "Are the logos ready?"

"Yep, I'll bring 'em in."

"Just leave them at your desk. I'll pick them up later."

"Sure thing." Lane turned and trotted off.

Samantha opened her mouth to speak, when Pam walked in the door. "Do you have a minute, Samantha? I need to go over this copy for the newsprint ads. Stuart has some crazy idea that—"

"How about if we talk after lunch, Pam?"

"Oh, sure, no problem." Pam backed out of the room, goggling at Jarrett.

Through all the interruptions, Jarrett waited patiently, but he never took his eyes off Samantha. Brenda waited, too, her eyes wide, darting back and forth between them. After Pam left, Samantha thrust the bouquet of flowers at Brenda.

"Would you please put these in water for me?"

Brenda nodded and finally took the hint. "Sure, Sam." She buried her nose in the blooms. "Mmm, lovely," she said and waddled out of the office.

"So, where are we going for lunch?"

"Nowhere," Samantha retorted and spun past him to close her office door. She didn't want this conversation overheard by anyone. "You shouldn't have come here, Jarrett."

"I wanted to apologize. I was wrong to say anything about Boomer. You were right to get angry. Family comes first."

"Okay," she said warily, surprised by his tack. "You didn't have to come here to say that."

"I leave Saturday for training camp," he said with a shrug. "I wanted to see you and to apologize in person."

This was *good* news. Jarrett Corliss would be out of her life and no longer such a temptation. By the time he returned, they would both have moved on to other things, other people. And once the season started, he would have much more to occupy his life than coaxing her to go out with him.

"Well, good luck. I hope it goes well."

"Me, too," he agreed. "Will I see you again before I leave?"

Regret flooded through her. "No."

He nodded. "I thought you'd say that." His deep blue gaze was level and direct. "I still disagree. And I'm not giving up on this."

"Jarrett—"

In one smooth motion, he stepped closer and slipped his arms around her. His mouth dropped to cover hers as he drew her firmly into his embrace. This was no soft, light kiss. This time, he held nothing back. His lips demanded a response from her. And they got it. Samantha was helpless to do anything but give him what he wanted—what she wanted, too.

He plundered her mouth with his, nibbling her lips and thrusting his tongue in to dance with hers. Samantha's arms rose to encircle his neck, as he pulled her closer to his hard, muscled body. The image of him in a damp towel came flooding into her head. He felt even better than she had imagined. One calloused hand rose to tangle in her hair, and he tilted her head back so his lips could trace a path down her throat. Samantha shivered to feel the rasp of his whiskers against the sensitive, soft skin of her neck. He nuzzled into the vee of her blouse, then kissed his way across the cotton to the pebbled hardness of her nipple, evident through the layers.

Samantha was lost to sensation. When he arched her hips to his and rubbed against her in a slow, deliberate motion, she moaned softly in the back of her throat. Both of them were breathing hard. Jarrett raised his head and stared down at her, blue eyes nearly black with desire.

"I'm *not* giving up on you, Sammy," he vowed softly.

Samantha looked back at him, held motionless as much by the look in his eyes as by his strong grip. She shook her head slowly and tried to pull away, but Jarrett held her firm. She swallowed, searching for her voice.

"Let me go," she whispered through swollen lips. "This was a mistake. *I* made a mistake."

"It's no mistake," he insisted, giving her a slight shake. "You can't deny what we have—this desire—and I don't want to. Especially now."

Samantha squirmed, but he was unyielding. "Jarrett—"

He brushed his lips against her one more time, a delicate touch when their bodies still strained together. "Remember. It's not over. It's just begun."

With that, Jarrett released her. Samantha sat abruptly on the stool at her worktable. Her legs were wobbly and she didn't trust them to bear her weight. Jarrett walked to the door, then turned and looked back at her. She straightened her blouse, trying to regain her professional demeanor. It was difficult to do when his eyes twinkled mischievously at her.

"Please go," she said. "I have work to do."

"Miss me, will you, Sammy?"

"I doubt it," she said acidly.

Jarrett laughed and opened the door. Behind it, Brenda had a hand up as if to knock. She started, looking first at Jarrett, then at her boss, gaping to see Samantha so disheveled.

"Dietrich is on line one," she said faintly. "Should I—"

"Mr. Corliss is just leaving," Samantha said.

"But I'll be back. See you in six weeks."

He slipped past Brenda, and Samantha dropped her head into her hands. *How had she let that happen?*

"Sam?" Brenda asked. "Should I tell Dietrich you'll call him back?"

Samantha raised her head to meet her friend's worried eyes. She smiled unconvincingly. "No. I'll talk to him."

"Okay." Brenda hesitated, then finally offered, "Sam, if you need to talk, I'm here."

Taking a deep breath, Samantha gathered her composure. Jarrett Corliss was out of her life now. It was time to start forgetting him. She stood and walked over to her desk. As she lifted the phone, she looked at her friend. "The Rainiers leave for training camp Saturday. That means my problem is as good as gone."

"Really?"

"Yes. Positively," Samantha vowed. Six weeks was enough time for her to forget one man. She pushed the button to connect line one. "Dietrich. How are you?"

Chapter Seven

For three weeks, Emerald Advertising ran at top speed getting the Rainiers ready for their public debut. The new logo with its distinctive red-and-navy-blue crest was approved. Updated uniforms were tailored, stitched and rushed to the spring training camp just in time for the first preseason game. A short commercial spot aired with professional models sporting the new look. A local department store also had a fashion show featuring team memorabilia. The sharp new caps and jackets sold out within an hour after the show.

The first commercial debuted in Andrew Elliott's office. He leaned forward in his chair, watching intently. Samantha ignored the screen in favor of catching the older man's reactions. Besides, she had already seen it a dozen times by then. His only expression was a frown. What did that mean? Samantha held her tongue and waited. It was a very long sixty seconds. The music rose in a dramatic crescendo, and the screen faded to black. There was silence, then Elliott sat back, slapped his knee and hooted with laughter.

"That's a dilly! A real dilly." He turned to Samantha, shaking a finger at her. "You get that on the air as soon as possible," he ordered happily. "And while you're at it, make me another one just as good."

Samantha smiled and breathed a sigh of relief. "Yes, sir. It would be my pleasure."

News about the Rainiers began to show up in the sports section of the local newspapers. Luckily, the players failed to make news anywhere *but* the sports section. The first exhibition game was played on a Thursday and televised on a cable sports network. Brenda suggested to Samantha that they watch together.

"What a great idea. Why don't you come to my place? Since Craig is out of town."

"That sounds good," Brenda agreed. "I'll bring the pretzels and ice cream."

"Pretzels and ice cream?" Samantha laughed.

"You won't really appreciate the combination until you get pregnant," Brenda joked, patting her well-rounded tummy. "You supply the pizza."

"With or without anchovies?"

"Hmm, ice cream and anchovies. Sounds delicious."

So, Thursday evening they spread themselves on Samantha's couch, food heaped on the coffee table in easy reach. While they watched the game, Brenda picked and ate the anchovies off the pizza Samantha had ordered, alternating salty bits of fish with spoons of praline ice cream. Samantha shuddered and turned down Brenda's generous offer to share.

Samantha surprised herself by becoming completely engrossed in the game. She alternately cheered and chewed her fingernails as the team's prospects changed inning by inning. Having a stake in the team's success engaged her.

Brenda could only laugh at her intensity. "Sam, if you keep chewing at your nails like that you're going to lose both arms. This is only an *exhibition* game. Wait 'til the real season before you nibble so much."

"Hey, I thought all true fans sweated over their team's chances, even in the preseason games."

"Suddenly you're a fan," Brenda said. "I thought baseball bored you. What changed your mind—or should I ask *who?*" she added with a grin.

"Brenda, just shut up and watch the game. My interest in the Rainiers is strictly a matter of business."

"Ha!" Brenda snickered.

Samantha was spellbound when Jarrett's face filled the screen, and her heart skipped in a little dance of excitement. She could see the determination to succeed—to win—in every inch of his body. In all their encounters, she had only seen him this focused, this intent, at one endeavor—kissing her. The idea that she could ignite such passion in him sent a tingle of pleasure down her spine. But there could not be anything between them. Samantha was glad when the camera panned back to show the entire infield from a distance.

Jarrett wound up for the pitch. He released the ball, and the batter swung for a strike. The catcher lobbed the ball back to Jarrett. He wound up for the second pitch. Quickly, he fired the ball to first base where the runner was far from the bag, poised to steal second. The runner made it safely back to first, but he was warned and more cautious. Jarrett's second pitch only earned the batter a foul ball.

Samantha sat through the game, riveted to the screen, as was Brenda. The third inning finished with the Rainiers ahead by one. Then the big moment came. Samantha and Brenda screeched when their commercial began to play. Samantha turned the sound up, and they leaned forward, holding their breath as the spot unwound. It starred Jarrett and depicted how he got started pitching.

First a young, towheaded boy portrayed Jarrett as a kid on the family farm. In a picturesque rural scene that might be

Oklahoma, the boy worked on a haystack that was next to a barn. Dressed in only rolled-up dungarees, the barefoot boy tossed the hay skyward with a large pitchfork. As the camera drew back, it showed the boy was so good at pitching hay that instead of landing in the barn's loft, the hay flew over the roof and an even larger haystack had formed on the other side of the barn.

Then the scene switched to the real Jarrett, posed next to a haystack, pitchfork in one hand and dressed in the same type of rolled-up overalls the boy had worn. One strap hung loose, and half of his broad, muscular chest was exposed. The muscles rippled enticingly as, with his other hand, he lazily tossed a baseball into the air and caught it.

"Ya'll come see me pitching for the Rainiers on opening day. Y'hear?" he prompted in his low, sexy drawl.

Samantha felt a flush rise throughout her body. Every time she saw the commercial, she had the same reaction. The first time, screening it with the director, she had been thankful the room was darkened and her face was hidden. If the spot was half as effective with other women, the Rainiers would have the stadium filled in no time. Wives and girlfriends would fight their men to get a good seat.

The commercial concluded with the message: "The Seattle Rainiers—watch the new kids play a whole new game."

Brenda sat back as it ended, and a beer commercial flashed on the screen. Samantha muted the sound.

"Wow, Sam, you were one-hundred-percent right about that man's sex appeal. I mean, I know he's handsome and all, but I had no idea it would show so well on TV." Brenda fanned herself with her hand. "Hot stuff."

Samantha wasn't sure whether to accept Brenda's words as congratulations or rush out and pull the commercial off the air. Jarrett *was* hot. She had known that since the moment she met him. Now everyone else knew. The light, warm humor of the commercial coupled with the close-up shots of him would put him in high profile. Her company would get part of the credit. So why wasn't she happier? The game resumed, and she and Brenda were engrossed once again in the play.

"He's good. You know that?" Brenda asked as they watched Jarrett toss the ball to a relief pitcher coming from the bullpen. Jarrett had pitched four innings, a long stretch for an exhibition game.

"Yes," Samantha agreed. "He just might pull it off."

"What's going on with you two?" Brenda had not yet said a word about Jarrett's visit to the office. Nor had she commented on how rattled Samantha had been afterward.

"Nothing." Spying Brenda's doubtful look, Samantha added, "Really, there's nothing going on."

Brenda gave a snort of disbelief, her look one of skepticism, but didn't push the inquiry.

Samantha sighed. There *was* something between her and Jarrett. It was eating at her, keeping it all inside. There was no sense hiding it from Brenda, of all people.

"I don't know what to do with him, Bren. He won't leave it alone."

Brenda looked down at the cup she held, swirling the contents around the bottom. "Won't leave what alone?"

"This…this…whatever it is between us."

"What *is* it between you? You've been very tight-lipped about Jarrett since the first day you showed me his picture."

"I—" Samantha paused, at a loss for words. "I don't exactly know."

Brenda nodded. "Well, whatever it is, do you *want* him to leave it alone? To leave *you* alone?"

"Yes. No." Samantha threw her hands up in exasperation. "I don't know."

"So what *do* you want to do?"

"Smack him over the head with a baseball bat." Samantha laughed. "He has got the most irritating habit of ignoring what I say when it's the opposite of what he wants to hear."

Brenda chuckled. "That's just a male trait, sweetie. They're born with it. They can't help it." She paused, then added, "So what have you done about it?"

"Told him that I won't go out with him." She paused, debating, then admitted, "I did go out with him once. To dinner."

"You did? Why didn't you tell me?"

"I should have. I know." Samantha held up a hand in defense. "But he tricked me into it."

"*Tricked* you?" Brenda was incredulous.

"It was at the photo shoot. He *claimed* he was sick and wouldn't be in any of the last shots if I didn't go out with him."

"That's blackmail!"

"That's what I told him." Samantha shook her head, looking at her friend. "But what could I do? He had me. I only had that one day with Carl. Rescheduling was impossible."

Brenda shook her head in disbelief, but her tone was not very sympathetic. "That's really low, Sam. What a cad." Then she asked, "So how did the dinner go?"

"Too well. He wants to see me again. And he won't take no for an answer, either."

"That's terrible. I don't know *what* I'd do if a gorgeous ballplayer was pestering me like that."

Samantha gave her friend a dry, humorless look. "I'm glad you find it so amusing. But you forget the contract we have with Andrew Elliott, who's not so keen on gossip around his team—which my dating Jarrett could cause."

"Hmm, I see what you mean." Brenda thought for a moment. "Well, I still think you're nuts to pass up a guy as gorgeous as Jarrett Corliss, but if it's crucial to Elliott that you keep business and pleasure separate, then that's what you have to do. If Jarrett won't listen, just don't answer his calls. And if he shows up at the office, I can tell him you're busy or out.'

Samantha smiled gratefully. She should have confided in her friend earlier. She knew—had known all along—Brenda would keep her secret. With her help, maybe she could keep Jarrett at a distance.

The game wound to an end. The Rainiers lost by two. An ominous sign, even though it was only a preseason game. Samantha switched off the television.

"Well, Sam, not that it hasn't been an interesting evening, but I've got to go home." Brenda struggled to her feet. "Baby and I have got to get some beauty sleep."

Samantha rose to give her a hand. "Thanks for coming over, Brenda. I appreciate you listening to my woes."

"No problem. *I* should have the problems you have. If a man like Jarrett Corliss chased me with as much determination as he's chasing you, I don't think I'd run very fast or very far."

"Believe me, I sometimes feel like I should have my head examined for pushing him away. But he's off-limits as far as I'm concerned," she said firmly. "Besides, what do I want with an arrogant baseball player anyway?"

Samantha escorted her friend to her car.

"Well," Brenda said, hugging Samantha when they reached it, "if there's anything I can do, just let me know."

"Thanks." Samantha helped her get seated. "Good night. See you at work tomorrow."

Samantha returned to the warmth of her condo. She stacked the dishes and picked up the empty pizza box. When everything was tidy, she got ready for bed. For a while, she lay trying to read, but the effort was futile. Her thoughts kept turning to Jarrett.

Exasperated with herself, she turned off the light and settled down to sleep. Just as she was getting relaxed and drowsy, the phone rang. She sat up and turned the light on again.

"Hello?"

"Hi, Sammy."

Her heart jumped to triple its normal rhythm, speeding up as soon as his smooth drawl sounded across the miles of telephone line. "Jarrett? Are you all right?"

"I'm fine." His voice was low and sounded tired. "How are you, Sam?"

Samantha's mind scrambled to find words to make a coherent sentence. Hearing him so close in her ear and at such a late hour in bed made her thoughts whirl. "I'm fine. You sound tired."

"I'm more than tired."

"Is training rough?" Unconsciously, her voice had dropped to the same intimate level as his. She was concerned only with Jarrett, how he sounded, why he had called her from so far away.

"I tell you, it's a killer some days." He paused, then before Samantha could say anything, he continued, "Actually, it could be worse. We have the usual glitches to unravel. We're always worse than we think we'll be in practice. The first game went okay."

"I know. I saw it." Silence greeted this bit of information. "Brenda came over, and we watched it together. You pitched well, at least I thought so." She heard nothing from the phone for the longest time. Her heart pounded, waiting for him to speak. Finally she couldn't stand it any longer. "Jarrett? Are you still there?"

"Yes. Thanks for watching, Sammy. I appreciate that more than you know." His voice became more alive, warmer and husky.

"Well, I do have a vested interest in the team," she said, trying to diffuse the intimacy of his words.

"Is that what you call it? Vested interest?" he asked. She could tell by his voice he was smiling.

Samantha smiled in response, imagining his face. "Just make sure you keep doing well. I bet my company on you guys." As the tone of the conversation relaxed, so had Samantha. She sank into her pillow and twirled a lock of hair around her fingers.

Jarrett chuckled. "I'll do my best. I can't speak for the rest of the team, but I'd do just about anything for you, darlin'."

Was he still teasing? Samantha wasn't sure. She tensed. "Jarrett—"

"Anything except leave you alone, maybe."

"I've noticed you have a problem hearing the word 'no,'" she replied dryly.

"What was that you said, Sammy? I missed it. Phone must have a short in it."

She laughed. "Why did you call, Jarrett?"

"'Cause I miss you."

The simple words closed Samantha's throat with a lump of emotion. She swallowed hard. "You just miss our fights."

"Wrong. You want to know what I miss the most?"

A wealth of possibilities crowded her head and she swallowed hard. "No, I don't think that I do."

Jarrett chuckled. The sensual sound made her shiver, and she hugged her arms against her chest to ease the ache in her breasts. How could he make her body feel this way when he was so far away?

"I missed your voice, Sam. That's all. It's been a long day, and I wanted to talk to you."

Samantha paused, at a loss for words. "Well, I hope you weren't expecting me to start a fight tonight. It's too late, and I don't think I have it in me."

"Nope, no fight." He paused. "But now I know when to start a fight I want to win."

Samantha laughed. "Good night, Jarrett."

"'Night, Samantha. Sleep well."

"You, too." Samantha held the phone until she heard the click on the other end, so far away from her, then lowered her own.

She turned the light off again and lay with her eyes open in the darkness. Before them, she saw Jarrett's face. Why, just when she was getting her mind so neatly arranged, storing him safely away in the attic, did he come along and drag himself back into the living room? Tonight, when he was so sweet and funny, she had a difficult time keeping him in the proper place.

If he had been here in person, she would have gone into his arms willingly. When he was arrogant, telling her what was going to happen between them, she had little trouble resisting him. *Then,* she could easily pretend that she had not the slightest interest in him. At times like tonight, Jarrett easily entranced her. Why couldn't he be simple and predictable like all the other jocks she had known?

Samantha rolled over in the darkness and punched her pillow to fluff it. Sleep was a long time coming. When it did arrive, she dreamed about a baseball game. She was watching it through the gaps in some kind of fence. It was played in a huge stadium, which, try as she might, she could not enter.

Chapter Eight

The commercial featuring Jarrett doubled ticket sales overnight. Andrew Elliott was thrilled with the response. Samantha's company celebrated, then went on to produce another commercial that aired one week before the team returned to Seattle. This one, Pam and Carol's baby, featured a young Boomer hitting a home run that broke a stained-glass window in a church across town. The scene was immediately followed by a handsome, adult Boomer pounding one into the stands. The new commercial added to the furor bubbling around the team and fans clamored for more.

Emerald Advertising hummed along, churning out more ads for magazines and newspapers. Billboards were up throughout Seattle. The printers had started on the first batch of new programs. For Samantha and her crew, the volume of work increased tenfold, but the routine made it a bit easier. So far. Samantha crossed her fingers and hoped that all would stay smooth and only slightly hectic and not return to the stormy chaos of the first weeks.

The day before opening day, Samantha found herself pushing papers around her desk, getting nothing done. All her work came to fruition in less than twenty-four hours, when the fans swarmed the stadium for the first game. She and her team had done everything they could. Tomorrow, the Rainiers would have to take over and live up to their new image. The anticipation was driving her crazy, but opening day wasn't the only trial before her.

Jarrett was home.

Though she tried to squelch her excitement, the knowledge thrummed through her like a live wire. She hadn't heard from him. In fact, she had not spoken to him since that intimate phone call during training camp. Each time a preseason game aired, she watched, then waited for the phone to ring. She tried not to feel disappointed when he didn't call. She was being ridiculous. Why would she want him to call? Hadn't she decided that she shouldn't, couldn't and wouldn't talk to him anyway? Irritated with herself, she tried to push all thoughts of Jarrett Corliss out of her mind.

She dropped the file she had been trying to read and picked up another. Raised voices outside her office brought a welcome distraction. Samantha half rose, wondering what the excitement was all about. Before she could stand, Jarrett strode into the doorway with Debbie right behind him.

"Sir, you can't go in there!" Debbie was tugging at Jarrett's arm while he completely ignored her. "I'm sorry, Samantha," Debbie nearly wailed. "I tried to keep him out, but he wouldn't listen."

Samantha sat back down with a plop, momentarily breathless. She drank in the sight of him, tall and broad-shouldered. How could she have forgotten how handsome he was? All those hard muscles encased in denim and a knit sweater. Hair that begged to be touched, lips that would warm to her kisses. The dimple was missing though, and his eyes glittered with a message she could not interpret.

"It's all right, Debbie," Samantha soothed. "I'll handle Mr. Corliss."

Debbie backed away. "Are you sure?" she asked, with a glance at Jarrett's set face.

"I'm sure. Thanks."

Debbie nodded once, then turned and left. Samantha stood and faced him. "Jarrett?" Though she tried to keep her voice cool, she knew she failed dismally. The tremble of awareness was too evident. "Welcome back."

"Hello, Samantha," Jarrett said tersely. "We need to talk."

The coldness of his greeting helped Samantha get control of herself. "What about?"

"That commercial."

"What about the commercial? It's great, isn't it? It's generating tons of calls, and ticket sales are incredible."

"That's not all it's generating." Jarrett's expression was easy to decipher now: he was furious. This was not the tender lover she had last heard on the phone so many nights ago. "This afternoon, after practice, I was mobbed outside the stadium. I barely made it to my car alive."

"What—"

"Mobbed, Sam. By women. By *teenage girls!* Dammit, I'm a baseball player. That commercial makes me look like a countrified gigolo."

Samantha stared at him. She couldn't understand why he was so upset. "Jarrett, everyone loves that commercial. It's making a huge difference for the team. They—*you*—have got fans now. Advance ticket sales have never gone this well."

"I'll *bet* they've sold lots of tickets." He smiled grimly. "That little sixty-second spot damned near promises I'll personally screw every woman in the stadium."

"Jarrett, this is what everyone has been working for. If there are this many people buying tickets, profits increase. Elliott will keep the team. That means *you* have a job that lasts longer than one season."

"I won't be alive next season. Those female vultures you unleashed will tear me apart."

Samantha took a deep, calming breath and tried a different tack. "Listen, the excitement will die down after a week or so. That's how these things go. There's already another commercial out that features Boomer and a third is scheduled to air next week with Alvendia in it. In the meantime, just…I don't know, enjoy the attention."

"Enjoy it? Samantha, how am I supposed to enjoy women grabbing at me every time I walk outside? Asking me to dinner, for drinks—hell, one woman asked me to have her baby!" He crossed his arms and glared angrily at her. "I don't mind signing autographs, but this is ridiculous."

Samantha rubbed a hand across her forehead, reining in her frustration. "Take my advice. Just *ignore* them. You're the first Rainier on television. You won't be the last. The others will all get the same publicity and this first flurry will die down."

Jarrett snorted. "Yeah? And in the meantime, my life is trashed."

The phone buzzed. "Samantha? Dietrich is on line one. He says it's important."

"I'll be right with him." Samantha turned to Jarrett. "Look, there's nothing I can do about the commercial, even if I wanted to. Now, you'll have to excuse me. I need to take this call."

"Thanks a lot, Sam, great job." His tone was scathing. His blue eyes shot daggers at her once more before he turned on his heel and walked out. He shut the door behind him with a bang that rattled the glass.

Samantha stared after him in amazement. She had expected Jarrett to comment on the commercial, maybe offer up some praise. This rampage was completely unexpected. Slowly, she sat back down at her desk. She had feared that once the commercial aired, Jarrett would be besieged by offers from other women he couldn't—or wouldn't—refuse. Apparently, that was not going to be a worry. Just the opposite: he hated the attention Samantha had worked so hard to get him.

The blinking light on the phone beckoned. She picked it up and soothed the director's frazzled nerves. When she ended the call, she could still feel Jarrett's anger in the room. The more she thought about him, the more irritated she became. She and her company had pulled an advertising coup. Emerald Advertising had managed to transform the Seattle Rainiers from a public-relations nightmare to a dream team. She would not apologize for doing her job and doing it well. What had he expected? If he wanted to avoid the public—his *fans*—he shouldn't have left the farm.

Egotistical bastard.

Samantha rose and paced; her agitation wouldn't allow her to sit still. Who did he think he was, storming in here like that? All her tender thoughts about him burned up in the flames of her anger. All he had ever done was push her around. As if his were the only opinions and feelings to consider. Well, he could take his temper tantrum and stuff it. If this was the way he was going to behave, she was glad she had kept him at arm's length. Jarrett Corliss had pushed her around for the last time.

THE NEXT DAY, SAMANTHA'S anger had settled into determination. She was almost grateful for Jarrett's explosion. If he had offered her his passion, she would have been lost. She knew it. Instead, their confrontation reminded her where her duty lay. Thanks to Jarrett, her attention was focused right where it should be—on advertising the Rainiers. This was the most important day of the team's—and her company's—year.

Just after noon, everyone left the office. They needed no urging to get them to the ballpark early. Samantha checked her bag before she headed over to the stadium herself. She was as excited as anyone. She grabbed her blue-and-white striped sweater and slipped it over the white cotton blouse she wore. Navy linen slacks and low heels completed an outfit that was casual but still professional, and would blend in with the crowds.

On the street outside the Smith Tower, she caught a south-bound bus and joined the mass of people headed for the game. Judging by the proliferation of hats and shirts, all with a familiar logo, the team was at least earning a hefty income from merchandising. Six stops later, the bus was overloaded, its passengers squeezed to standing room only. One more stop and they reached the stadium.

Samantha took a deep breath and joined the crowds streaming toward the main gate. As she drew near the entrance, she saw a familiar face. Simultaneously, Peter Brinks spied her. He waved, and she walked to meet him.

"Peter, nice to see you again."

"Likewise, Miss James." He shook her hand. "Right this way."

As she had on her first visit, Samantha followed Peter Brinks into the mazelike stadium. This time they stuck to the upper tiers instead of diving into the nether regions that housed the locker rooms. Down a dark, narrow corridor, Samantha saw daylight glowing like a beacon. They fell in with others headed toward the same brightness. When they emerged at the end, they were hit with a wall of sound. The voices of happy, excited fans clashed with the organ music that blared through speakers. The shouts of vendors hawking beer, peanuts, popcorn and hot dogs completed the cacophony.

Samantha followed Peter on a contorted path up one set of stairs and halfway down another. He came to a private box— six seats enclosed by a waist-high wood rail and gate. It was directly behind home plate.

"Here you are, Miss James. Mr. Elliott will be here after the senator throws out the first ball. Enjoy the game." Peter turned away, then turned back. "Oops. I almost forgot." He handed her a plastic card on a cord. "This pass will get you into the corridor outside the locker room after the game." Then he was gone.

Samantha stepped into the box and chose a seat near the exit so she could slip in and out to survey the stands. Unlike the newer stadiums, Sicks still had old-fashioned, open boxes. No sky-view room, not even for the team's owner. Several women in nearby boxed seats eyed her curiously, but did not speak to her. Samantha ignored them and thumbed through her program. She glanced through the glossy pages, noting small things to review with the printer and improve. The ink seemed to be bleeding here and there on a few photos and graphics, but, overall, they had done an excellent job. She knew most of the programs were tossed away at the end of the game, but attention to detail, even on these disposable items, reflected on the team and on her company.

The stadium was filling fast. Red and blue clothing abounded. Samantha glanced at her watch: fifteen minutes before the start. Time enough for a quick walk around. Though she had been in the stadium the day before when crews were hanging the banners and signs, she wanted to assess the final creation in its full splendor, dancing in the breeze of the open-air stadium, floating over the milling crowds.

She strolled inside, along the upper tier where food stalls and beer stands lined one wall. Samantha was pleased by the look of the new decorations. The bright, fresh signs were clear and easily readable even with the numerous people filling the area. A sizable queue formed at the shop selling Rainiers paraphernalia. T-shirts and hats seemed to be favorites. Satisfied with her tour, Samantha threaded her way back through the jostling crowds to her seat.

As she came out of the darkness of the corridor and into the light, a single trumpet began to play the national anthem. Each sweet, clear note reverberated from the field to the stands, gaining power as it floated into the cloudless blue sky. Samantha stood, hand over heart until the end. Senator Ganssle threw out the first ball and the umpire yelled, "Play ball!" The season had begun.

Samantha felt lightness and excitement stir her soul. She hoped the Rainiers would do well enough this season so that there would be games like this for many years to come.

She returned to her seat and had just gotten settled when Andrew Elliott arrived. Before sitting down, he chatted with some other men and women in the seats nearby. Eventually he came to sit beside her.

"Everything looks great, Samantha. You've done a bang-up job." Tonight his cheeks were rosier than usual, his youthful vigor revved to a fever pitch.

"Thank you. It all looks pretty stylish, doesn't it? Your crew has been very good to work with."

"Yep, they did a class job. They better. I'm paying 'em enough," Elliott barked. "You'll be interested to know that we've sold more advance tickets for this season than all the tickets sold last year."

"That's wonderful!"

"Let's hope it keeps up. If we win this one, it would really start us out on the right foot." Elliott abruptly turned his attention to the game and conversation stopped.

Jarrett was the starting pitcher, and Samantha also found herself forgetting everything else but the game. Sitting behind home plate as she was, she could look at him directly, though she couldn't see his features clearly. Sometimes his face was magnified to colossal status on the scoreboard screen. The intensity of his expression reminded Samantha of that first exhibition game she and Brenda had watched. And she again remembered how his passion for baseball looked so similar to his passion when he had kissed her. Despite her anger, it sent a pang to her heart.

Three innings came and went, and the score was tied at two apiece before Samantha noticed that Mr. Elliott was no longer beside her. She looked around and spied him above and to the left of her, talking with a business associate, or so Samantha guessed. As she watched, he laughed, shook hands with the man and sat down in a vacant seat in another VIP box. He worked the stands like the consummate businessman he was.

Samantha recognized some of those to whom Elliott spoke. One man was also a client of Emerald Advertising. Across the aisle, she spotted a former boss of hers who was now a competitor. He came over and chatted about the ad business in general and congratulated her on her work with the Rainiers. After he returned to his seat, Samantha's attention was caught by the fans in the box in front of hers. These were a group of six women, unaccompanied by men. One she thought she recognized, a woman recently divorced from a wealthy computer company executive. Samantha had no compunction about leaning forward a bit to catch the gist of their chatter. After all, they were her target market.

They were all young and very beautiful. Definitely not typical baseball fans. As she watched, she noticed that they paid scant attention to the action on the field. They were supremely indifferent to the sport, but they all had an eye for baseball players. One player in particular seemed to dominate their conversation: Jarrett Corliss. Samantha thought of Jarrett's angry reaction to the women importuning him. Were these six some of the ones he complained about? Seeing them, Samantha wondered why he would refuse such perfection and grace. Women such as these would be a constant temptation for any man—these lovely, *willing* women.

A cheer went up from the stands and Samantha looked up in time to see Hank Wilson catch a pop fly. That ended the fourth inning. Samantha tried to ignore the women below her and watch the game. At the seventh inning stretch, she stood and sang "Take Me Out to the Ball Game" with the other thirty-two thousand fans. At the bottom of the seventh inning, Boomer came through for the Rainiers, sending a double hit into right field that gave Alvendia enough time to make it from second to home. The next batter popped out. The score was tied at three-all.

When the Rainiers came back on the field at the top of the eighth inning, Jarrett was not with them. The name of the relief pitcher was announced—Ben Rosenthal—but no more was said about the change. Samantha was not surprised. In fact, she was more surprised that the coach had kept Jarrett in so long for the first game of the season. She wondered if he was all right. He had pitched a long seven innings, and his shoulder was not at its best. She watched the game, but a vague worry lurked in the back of her thoughts. The eighth inning came and went. The Rainiers pulled ahead by one run.

IN THE LOCKER ROOM, below the thousands of fans still watching the game, Jarrett sat on a varnished wood bench. His Rainiers shirt hung on a hook behind him. One of the trainers massaged the muscles in and around his shoulder.

"How's he doin'?" the pitching coach asked. He had come down for a minute to check on Jarrett once the team was at bat.

"Marginal," was the reply. "He'll need to soak a while before we'll know more."

"You feel okay, Jarrett?"

"It's a little stiff," he admitted, then smiled confidently.

"But after Bill marinates me in his special meat tenderizer and beats it to a pulp, it'll be fit as a fiddle."

The coach grunted without amusement. "Give it a rest the next couple days. Keep it in a sling. I want you to start again Thursday." With a nod to the trainer, the coach marched back to the dugout.

The trainer finished the massage and wrapped Jarrett's arm in a sling. Stripping off his cleats, pants and socks one-handed gave Jarrett no trouble. He had perfected that feat while he recovered from his surgery a year ago. Naked, he padded across the locker room, past the steam room to the trainer's area and the large stainless steel whirlpool in the corner. Jarrett eased into the hot bath with a groan of pleasure, and Bill turned on the water jets.

"Keep that shoulder on those jets," Bill instructed. "I'll be back to take a look at it after a while."

Jarrett leaned back into the pulsing water. The heat and massage helped ease the pain immensely. He shouldn't have toughed out that last inning. This pain and the risk were not worth it. He closed his eyes and listened to the game that was echoing through the loudspeakers in the locker room. The eighth inning ended with the Rainiers up one.

Unconsciously, Jarrett held his breath at each pitch, willing his replacement and his other teammates to hold it together. They did. The top of the ninth passed and the opposing team didn't score. The game was over. Even without the speakers, Jarrett could hear the deafening roar of victory filter from the stadium into the therapy room when the last batter struck out. A surge of adrenaline pumped through him as the team streamed in to the locker room. Their spirits and his were running high. Exhibition season had gone decently, but this first real victory gave them high hopes.

"Hey, Jarrett. Way to throw the ball, *compañero,*" Alvendia shouted, his voice echoing off the tiled walls. The burly right fielder gave him a high five and turned to pound another teammate on the back. Jarrett laughed as he watched the antics of his teammates. Happiness was like a drug they had all taken, as they whooped and hollered their elation. Bill came back, turned the jets off and ordered him to the showers. Jarrett's shoulder felt worlds better, but he wasn't sure if it was the massage, the whirlpool or the win that did the job.

A sea of people flooded the locker room: reporters, cameramen, staff members and anyone else who could sneak past security. They all jostled for positions next to the players. They wanted to talk to them, touch them, or just be near them in the hope that winning might be contagious.

Coming from the showers, with just a towel wrapped around his hips, Jarrett found several microphones thrust brutally into his face.

"Hey, Corliss. How does it feel to have your first win of the season?"

"How's your arm?"

"What do you think was the determining factor in tonight's win?"

The questions were trite and familiar. Jarrett had been hearing them, or variations of them, thrown at one player or another for his entire career. He answered the questions dutifully and, eventually, they found other game to hunt. He pulled on jeans and a shirt, socks and shoes, combed his hair and grabbed his jacket out of his locker. Before he put on his jacket, he slipped on the sling the coach had ordered him to wear. He dodged his way around the horde and edged out of the locker room without being noticed.

Outside, the corridor was cool and relatively quiet. From the direction of the stands, the glare of daylight shone down the dim corridor. Limned in the glow, a woman stood in sil-

houette as she spoke to two other figures. Jarrett knew it was
Samantha. Like a spirit drawn to heaven, he walked toward
her and the light that spilled around her. As he neared her, he
recognized the two other men from his visit to her office. He
ignored them and concentrated on her.

"Samantha."

She started when he said her name, but when she turned
to look at him, her face was controlled. And as beautiful as
always. Despite his anger, she still had the power to shake
him.

"Hello, Jarrett. Congratulations on your win."

"Yeah, it was great!" one of the guys with her said. He held
out a hand, which Jarrett shook with his left, since his pitching
arm was in the sling. "I'm Lane Marshall. This is Stuart Glick."

The other man shook Jarrett's hand as well. "Great
game, man."

"Thanks." Jarrett smiled. "Glad you enjoyed it."

"You'll take care of those items, Lane?" Samantha asked,
breaking into their circle. Both Lane and Stuart nodded as if
their heads were connected by an invisible string. "Okay, I'll
see you tomorrow."

With that, she turned away, but Jarrett grabbed her by the
arm. "Great to meet you guys, but I need a few words with
your boss."

The two men beamed as Jarrett led Samantha farther down
the corridor toward the stands.

"What is it?" Samantha asked, tugging her arm out of his grip.

"We need to talk."

Samantha laughed, a short, harsh sound. "What? Now you
want to talk? I thought we had graduated to yelling."

"I was talking then, Sam. *Not* yelling," he said impatiently.
"What are you going to do about that commercial?"

"Nothing. Andrew Elliott likes it. The public *loves* it, so it's running as is." She crossed her arms, stepping away from him. "Besides, I don't have any say about it. You'll have to talk to Elliott."

"But you could influence him, and you know it."

"Well, I don't want to. I told you before, just wait a week or two and it will all blow over." She turned to make her getaway. He followed as she skipped up a few steps and out another corridor.

"Wait, Samantha. I'm not done." She was rapidly approaching the door where a green exit sign glowed. Beyond that Jarrett knew he would be unable to follow her. He grabbed her by the arm. "Don't open that door."

"Why not?"

"Because you have no idea what I put up with just getting to my car every day."

"What you are talking about? Now, if you'll please let go of me."

"Look, I've dealt with groupies before. They're like a passel of hounds after a raccoon. I know that. But what's on the other side of that door goes way beyond that."

"You're a big boy. I'm sure you can handle it."

"Samantha, this is insane. My life has been taken over by these crazy women. Every time I leave the stadium there are so many flashbulbs going off, it's like the fourth of July. I had to have my phone number changed to another unlisted one after it started ringing all night long. Some of them already know where I live. I'll probably have to move to a hotel soon."

Samantha freed her arm and took a few more steps toward the door. "Come on, Jarrett, it can't be that bad. And I promise you, it will die down once the other commercials air."

With that, Samantha escaped through the double doors to the parking lot. Jarrett saw red. She couldn't just walk away from him; she had to fix this mess. Foolishly, he slammed through the door behind her.

As soon as they saw him, the fans surged forward. He was mobbed before he got two steps from the doors. The win had brought a larger than usual crowd. Of course, most of them were female. Samantha slipped through their ranks gracefully as they began screaming and crushing forward. He tried to follow her, but a wall of bodies blocked his path. Voices assailed him from all sides and made no sense at all. Programs and pens were pushed under his nose. The flash of cameras went off inches from his eyes. Hands reached out to touch him, hold him, grope him. He didn't know how many times he was kissed and squeezed. One girl grabbed onto the sling that cradled his arm. A stab of pain shot through his shoulder as she pulled herself up to kiss his cheek. Finally, with a strong push and the help of a police officer, Jarrett made it to his car. Three policemen held the crowd at bay until he backed out of his parking space and drove away. He pushed the accelerator down as hard as he dared. He had to stay on Samantha's trail and elude any fans that might try to follow him.

Samantha wasn't at her condominium when Jarrett arrived. He sat in his car waiting for her, his temper becoming more frayed by the minute. When she drove up, he jumped out of his car and grabbed her by the arm. "Stop running away. We have to talk about this, Samantha."

"We did talk." She snatched her arm away from him. "I said no, and you refused to listen. Give it up. You're not going to get your way this time. Now leave me alone!"

She stormed away. He stalked after her, catching up just as she unlocked her front door. This was not a fight he was going to lose. He grabbed her waist, pushed open the door and herded her into the entry.

"What are you doing?" she screeched.

"Making you talk to me." He slammed the door closed behind them.

"Jarrett!" She wriggled out of his grasp and reached for the door handle. "Leave."

Jarrett blocked her efforts to open the door. "No. I'm staying until you understand what that commercial is doing to me."

Without taking his eyes off hers, he wrenched off his jacket and the sling with it. Somehow, his shoulder didn't bother him so much now. As he stalked toward her, Samantha backed away until they were in the living room.

"Did you see what it was like outside the stadium after the game?" he demanded. "Did you see the mob?"

"Yes, but—"

"But nothing. It's like that everywhere. I walk down the street and girls want to kiss me. I've been propositioned so many times, I've lost count."

Samantha let out a sharp sound of disgust. "You are a baseball player, Jarrett. You're supposed to have fans."

Jarrett ran a frustrated hand through his hair, knowing he wasn't getting through to her. "Samantha, I knew I'd have my share of the spotlight. That's part of the game. I can accept that. What I can't accept is the way you've portrayed me in those damned ads."

"What?" She frowned. "You're a pitcher. That's how you're portrayed."

"No. That commercial's got nothing to do with baseball, except that I happen to be tossin' one in my hand." Jarrett's drawl became more pronounced, the more agitated he got. "And on the billboards I've seen, I look like I'm wearin' damn near nothin' but a smile." He began to pace. "And why am I the only one on all those billboards? What about the rest of the team?" He paused, just inches from her, searching her eyes. "I'm not askin' for anything other than what's fair. I know the team needs publicity, but why am *I* the only one being exposed? And why do I look like fresh meat waitin' to be slaughtered in every single ad?"

"Oh, this is so typical," Samantha fumed. "What is it with you jocks? Your arrogance is amazing." She gritted her teeth, her anger icy now. "You are *not* the only guy in the spotlight. Every other player has, or will, get the same exposure. You are just the first."

Jarrett was stunned. She wouldn't admit she was using him. She didn't care that his life was a misery because of her advertising campaign. Why? What was she up to?

"Sam, you *are* treating me differently, whether you admit it or not. Is this some sort of scheme to keep me at a distance?"

"What? That's ridiculous."

"No, it's not," he countered. The idea blossomed in his head so clearly that it had to be the truth. "You think, because I've chased you, that I'm like that with every woman. So, you set this up to teach me a lesson."

"No!"

"From the start, you've denied your feelings for me. You used your business, your brother, Elliott, anything you could to do it. Now you're using these ads."

"Jarrett, this is absurd."

"And I tricked you into a date. Are you getting back at me for that, too?" Jarrett locked his eyes on hers. "What are you really afraid of?" he asked softly.

She ignored his question, raising her chin a notch. "Are you finished?"

Jarrett reached out and grabbed her shoulders. His voice came out low and intense. "Almost. So pay attention. I'm only going to say this once. Nothing and no one, not even this ad, and certainly not all the women propositioning me, is going to keep me from having you. Understand?"

Samantha's eyes were still cold. "Thanks for the warning, Jarrett. I've had enough. Get out."

She tried to jerk free of his grasp, only to be drawn closer. It had been too long since he had held her in his arms. The scent of her alone drove him to the edge—sweet, sweet woman. He needed her so badly, especially now. He dropped his face to her hair, savoring the softness while drawing in her perfume.

"No, Sam. You haven't had nearly enough," he whispered into her hair. He sighed. It was almost a groan. "I know I haven't. I don't think I ever will." His lips brushed softly over hers. "I missed you. I haven't even told you that yet. Did you know I forced myself *not* to call you after that first time at camp? Hearing your voice just made me miss you more."

He had wanted her so badly for what seemed like forever. He didn't want to hear her arguments anymore. The kiss that followed started gentle, but it didn't stay that way. First Jarrett's tongue came out to tease her lips, begging for admittance. Samantha opened her mouth to him, reluctantly, shyly. Their tongues touched, darted away like timid creatures, then touched again. It was a ritual, and a precursor to more. All the anger they had felt melted into an urgent hunger for each other.

Jarrett couldn't be satisfied with just tasting her lips. He had to have more. All of her. His lips left hers and cruised over her face, sampling her every feature from nose to eyebrow to the soft skin under her chin. He nibbled his way to her ear, then down her throat. Samantha's head dropped back, offering him anything he chose to sample.

His hands delved beneath the sweater she wore, slipping buttons from their holes and easing the knit fabric off her shoulders. Her blouse still stood as a barrier to his fingers and lips, but Jarrett could not resist cupping and molding the fullness beneath it. His admiring gaze absorbed the erotic image of his hands against her breasts, her head thrown back in abandon. When her nipples prodded his palms, his fingers sped to the buttons that would free them.

Once more, his mouth found the soft skin that he adored and he trailed kisses down into the perfumed cleavage between the cups of her bra. Lace rasped against his tongue as he found and laved his prizes. The scent of her was overwhelming to the senses.

Jarrett raised his head. "Let me love you, Samantha," he whispered against her lips. "Here. Now."

Samantha shivered at his words and her eyelids lifted slowly. Her lips were swollen from his kisses, and Jarrett could not resist pressing yet another to their plump sweetness.

"Please."

"Jarrett." Her voice was husky. "I want you—" What she would have added was lost as he responded to those three little words. His heart raced in elation. She wanted him as much as he wanted her. She would surrender to the passion between them. As he pulled her closer, she pushed her hands against his chest, wrenching her mouth from his.

"No." Her voice was a soft plea. "I can't do this."

"Sammy?" Jarrett's voice was low and urgent.

"I'm sorry," she whispered, tears welling up and spilling over her lashes, tracing silvery streaks down her cheeks. "I can't do this," she repeated. "There's too much at risk."

Jarrett bent his head and looked down at all he had exposed. He squeezed his eyes shut and, slowly, rested his forehead on her shoulder. His breath came hard as he fought for control. Samantha raised a hand to touch his hair, but he jerked away, turning his back to her.

"Is this more of the lesson?" he asked harshly, turning back to face her.

She was fumbling to button her blouse. "This has nothing to do with revenge."

He caught and held her gaze with his own. "I feel like I'm being used, Sam," he said softly. "Am I just a product for you to promote?"

"No!" she cried. "I kissed you—" She stopped, wrapping her arms around herself. "You have to go now. Please."

"What's your game?" he demanded.

She flinched as if he had struck her. "I'm not playing games."

Determination welled up inside him. He walked forward, holding Samantha with his eyes. He didn't touch her again with his hands or body, but he pressed a kiss to her lips.

"I'm not, either," he warned her quietly.

Her eyes met his. "It's over, Jarrett."

Jarrett smiled. "It hasn't even begun."

Samantha shook her head, but she didn't speak. Jarrett walked to the door and opened it. He looked back down the short hallway, seeing her framed in the arched opening.

"We're just getting started, Samantha. Just wait."

Chapter Nine

Samantha tossed another pink message slip into the trash. The pile of them on her desk was reduced to three now, twenty fewer than when she had started. It was an achievement that would not last. Every time she left her office, even for lunch or a brief meeting, the stack grew again. She shouldn't complain. Many of the messages were from companies that wanted her firm to work for them.

Word of their success with the Rainiers had spread quickly. Some of these potential clients were getting rather insistent that Emerald promote their product or service. Samantha felt as if she had spent more time talking with potential clients in the past week than she had in the whole three years Emerald had been open.

She had made a quick trip to San Francisco to a clothing retailer, followed by an afternoon in Portland on the way back to meet an executive from a software company. She had also had two different dinner meetings with companies based in Seattle that had begun to court her. If she wasn't careful, she might easily contract more work than her small company could possibly handle. No more generic auto-parts fliers. From now on, it was BMW all the way.

So here she sat, on yet another afternoon, returning calls

and making appointments. Samantha slipped off her shoes, wiggled her toes into the carpet, then sighed. With all her messages, one person never called—Jarrett. After a week of silence, she should be used to it, but the knowledge that he had finally given up sent a pang of regret through her heart. Despite his words to the contrary, it was finally over between them. She should be happy. So why was she sitting here brooding? Samantha picked up the next message in one hand and the phone in the other. It was time for her to start forgetting.

The rest of the day sped by, as did the next, Friday. Emerald hummed along without any crises, and Samantha was happy to see the weekend stretch before her with no work to do. She walked on the beach and caught up on her sleep. She went to dinner with friends who had invited a charming, handsome man to partner her. She missed Jarrett's teasing drawl, though she repeatedly denied it to herself. Sunday night, she was just as glad to have the weekend over. Maybe work would keep thoughts of the irritating, arrogant, attractive pitcher out of her mind.

Monday morning, as Samantha passed the front desk, Debbie handed her a new stack of messages.

"Good morning," Debbie sang out, a bit too cheerfully. "Did you have a good weekend?"

"It was fine."

"Catch any baseball games?"

"No, I didn't." Samantha eyed her grinning receptionist. "My, aren't we in a good mood this morning."

"Of course," Debbie said, smothering a giggle behind one hand.

The phone rang, demanding Debbie's attention. Samantha headed to the back office. As she walked through the main room, Lane and Stuart each greeted her.

"'Mornin', boss-lady," Lane said with a grin.

"Wow! Fabulous suit," Stuart chimed in, a smile on his face, too. "A real heartbreaker."

"Thanks," Samantha answered, glancing at them quizzically. They seemed to have heard the same joke that Debbie had. "Though you've seen it before."

"Yeah? Well, it looks even better on you today," Lane assured her.

Samantha shook her head and went to her own office. Their snickering followed her. What were they up to now? Some sort of practical joke, she supposed, which she would soon discover. She passed Brenda's desk and received yet another undisguised smirk from her assistant.

"Why do I feel like Alice in Wonderland and that you've all turned into Cheshire cats?" Samantha wondered aloud.

Brenda's smirk turned into a laugh. "You haven't seen today's paper yet, have you?"

"No. Why?"

"You might want to look at the sports section," Brenda gurgled, hardly containing her glee. "And you'd better sit down before you read it."

"Why? What's go—"

Brenda steered her toward her office and pointed to the chair. When Samantha was seated, Brenda spread the morning's sports page on the desk in front of Samantha. There, in bold-faced type, was the headline Just a Lovesick Fool. A picture of Jarrett accompanied it.

"What is this?"

"Read it, Sam. It's… Well, it's something you have to read to believe." Brenda lowered herself into one of the chairs facing the desk, watching Samantha closely.

Samantha frowned at Brenda, then picked up the paper. She scanned the first sentence, then read the next more carefully, not quite believing the words. She felt herself go hot, then cold, then hot again. When she finished, she read the article through a second time, just to be sure she had not lost her mind.

"Oh my God," she breathed, horrified. "This can*not* be happening. Tell me this is not happening, Bren."

Brenda giggled aloud. "No can do, Sam. Craig read it to me this morning over toast and coffee. I just about died."

"*You* just about died? How do you think *I* feel?" Samantha's stunned eyes raced over the article a third time.

It seemed that Jarrett had told a reporter in Pittsburgh that he was pining away for the woman of his heart, Samantha James, and that she had refused to return his affections. The article went on to quote that she was the light of Jarrett's life, the only woman for him, yet she had spurned him. Samantha rubbed her temples and looked again. Yes, there was the word *spurned* in black ink.

"Well, I guess the cat's out of the bag now, isn't he?" Brenda commented.

Samantha glared at her friend. "Not one more remark, Brenda, or I'm going to sell your baby to the gypsies as soon as I can get my hands on it."

Brenda clapped a hand over her mouth to stifle the giggles that erupted at Samantha's threat. She got herself under control when Samantha did not join in her laughter. "Oh, come on. It *is* funny, you know."

"Not to me it isn't. If Elliott sees this—and I can't think of one reason he won't—our fish is fried."

This sobered Brenda as nothing else had. "Maybe he won't see it."

Samantha snorted. "And maybe hippos will sprout wings and fly over the moon."

She continued to stare at the paper, furious that Jarrett would pull such a stunt. He still wasn't taking no for an answer. The arrogance of the man was astonishing. Once again, he was going after what he wanted, regardless of the consequences. She felt a headache start as she thought about the possible repercussions. Elliott would be furious. How would she mollify him?

"Maybe Elliott won't care," Brenda said, drawing Samantha out of her gloomy thoughts.

"Do you really think that's likely?"

"Well, no," Brenda agreed. Then she brightened. "Maybe if you called him and told him it was a publicity stunt? Sort of a joke?"

"I don't think he'd see the humor in it, Bren." In one furious motion, Samantha crumpled up the newspaper and shoved it into the trash can. If only she could do the same with Jarrett's head.

The rest of that day, Samantha waited for Andrew Elliott's call with fear and trepidation. She tensed every time the phone rang. When she had to leave for a meeting across town, she dreaded the messages that would await her return. The first thing she did when she got back was shuffle through the pink slips frantically. Nothing. There were calls from everyone under the sun. Some messages referred to the article, some were oblivious to it, but not one from the owner of the Rainiers. Maybe he was too mad to talk to her.

The next day, Samantha picked up the paper herself and turned to the sports section, hoping in vain for a retraction. The story was the same, only in greater detail, than the day before. This time Jarrett lamented that Samantha's green eyes "were like shards of ice, piercing his soul." He went on to verify that her kiss—the one measly kiss she had given him—"was pure paradise." The hope of that paradise kept him going.

"No!" she shrieked. "What are you doing to me, Jarrett?"

Wednesday's edition was the worst yet. Jarrett's woes in wooing her became a more intricate, sorry tale with each installment. Samantha read about herself. She sounded more and more like some sort of love assassin—a cold woman with a heart cast in stainless steel. The story wasn't always the sports headline, but it was always on the front page of that section. She was incensed.

Over the course of three days, the story had turned the office upside-down and inside-out. The phone rang constantly, mostly calls from reporters who wanted an interview with her. Samantha felt like barricading herself in her office and ripping the phone jack out of the wall. She refused to speak to them and threw out all their messages as soon as they dropped on her desk.

Business meetings that had once been such a balm to her ego became torturous. Everyone wanted to know about her romance with Jarrett. Why had she turned him down? He seemed like a nice guy, didn't he? Handsome, with a good job, good prospects? Why didn't she like him? They all wanted to know the answer to one question: when was she going to relent and give the pitcher a chance?

To her surprise—and continuing anxiety—Andrew Elliott didn't call. The silence was ominous, and very unlike the direct, hard businessman she had come to know. Why was he holding back? Samantha found herself considering Brenda's suggestion seriously: maybe he had not heard the news. She could hope. Or maybe he had heard and assumed it *was* a publicity stunt. She even picked up the phone and dialed his number once or twice to talk to him. Both times she put the phone down before a connection was made. If he hadn't heard the story, she wasn't going to tell him. If he had…Well, she didn't want to wish him ill, but maybe the shock had at least incapacitated him for a while.

One other person hadn't called, either. Jarrett. He was smart enough to keep his distance. Samantha spent hours thinking of ways to retaliate. Public hanging was too good for him. In the end, she knew her hands were tied. If she denied the story to the reporters, it would only get more traction. Whatever she said, Jarrett would counter with something else. Probably something crazier, if that were possible. As frustrated as inaction made her, Samantha knew waiting was the wisest thing to do. Wait for Jarrett to come home. In the meantime, she would polish the silver platter on which she would place his head.

Chapter Ten

Samantha read the latest installment of Jarrett's woes in the Thursday morning edition of the newspaper. The article was short, just a recap of what he had already said, but it made her blood boil. She took a black-ink pen from the drawer of her desk and drew horns, fangs and crossed eyes over Jarrett's picture. Childish acts, she knew, but satisfying nonetheless. She flipped the newspaper closed and tossed it into the trash can. What a way to start the day.

A new stack of message slips stared up at her. She ignored them. She was in no mood to deal with business calls that were inevitably a ruse to probe about her and Jarrett. Samantha's temper was so frayed that it was a stretch to be merely civil— forget polite—to anyone. This morning she would be too tempted to tell everyone to keep their big, inquisitive noses out of her personal life.

Instead of making calls, Samantha concentrated on drafting a proposal for a potential client. A discount retail chain wanted to completely revamp itself. Its mom-and-pop, small-town image would be completely transformed into one more suited to the upscale, suburban market the company wished to penetrate. The company's management had big plans. They were adding twelve new stores in key southwestern states, and going public to raise capital. This job would be a plum, and she was so close to securing a deal, she could taste it.

Samantha was deeply engrossed in numbers, words and ideas when she was distracted by a soft knock on her open office door. She raised her head, eyes widening at the sight of Jarrett Corliss standing in the doorway, and bolted to her feet. Blond hair gleaming, dressed in his usual blue jeans and leather jacket, he was as handsome as ever. Her heart raced as all the fury of the past few days came rushing back.

"Hi, Sammy. Miss me?"

"How did you get in here?"

"Debbie said I should just come on back," he said with a lazy grin, moving into the room and swinging the door shut behind him. "She didn't tell you I was on my way?"

"No," Samantha said tartly. "She didn't mention you were here."

"Maybe she thought it was supposed to be a surprise." Unperturbed by her coldness, Jarrett perched on the corner of her desk, swinging a leg nonchalantly. "You look good, darlin'," he added. He made a lazy assessment of her from head to toe. "I take that back. You look better than good, Sammy. You look incredible."

Samantha ignored his caressing eyes. She felt an urge to gouge the dimple out of his face with her letter opener. His gall astounded her. How dare he waltz in here as if nothing had happened.

"So you've come to gloat. Is that it?" Samantha muttered between clenched teeth. It took all her will to keep her voice at a reasonable level.

"Gloat? No. I just got back in town. I had a hunch you'd want to see me."

"Oh, I want to see you all right. You have to stop these lies you've been telling."

Jarrett grinned, dimple prominent in one lean cheek. "Lies? Why, I've been telling the truth, Sammy. Don't you know full disclosure is the best way to avoid a scandal? So, I've been, ah—disclosing."

The cocky reply was just what she expected, but Samantha was still aggravated to no end. "How could you do this to me? To my company?"

"Do what? All I've done is tell the world what I've been telling you ever since we met. Now they all know that I'm a one-woman man. They also know that you're that one woman."

Samantha stalked around her desk, keeping her distance from him, and pointed to her office door. "Get out. This *one* woman has said no. Repeatedly," she roared. "Your arrogance is beyond belief, Jarrett. Is getting back at me this important? Is *your* need for revenge so great that you want me publicly humiliated?"

"Now hold—"

"I know why you did what you did," Samantha raged on. "This is my punishment for that commercial."

Jarrett moved so fast, she couldn't dodge his touch. His hands were on her shoulders in a moment and she jerked away, pressing her back to the door. He caged her there, one hand on either side of her head, but he didn't try to touch her again.

He wasn't smiling now. "It's not about that stupid commercial. I told my story to the public so that you would change your mind about me, about *us.*"

"Well, it worked. Instead of just *thinking* you're a manipulative bastard, now I *know* you are one."

Jarrett shook his head, his smile appearing once again. This only served to annoy Samantha further.

"Samantha, can't you—"

"No," she stopped him. "I don't want to hear any more. I just want you to stop. I get calls all day long from reporters and God knows what other weirdos. You've had your fun. Retract your story and leave me alone." She moved as fast as he had, ducking under his arm and taking refuge behind her desk. "And get out of my office!" The intercom buzzed. "What?" she barked.

"Mr. Elliott is on line two," Debbie said meekly.

Samantha felt a clutch of panic. She sank into her chair. "Thanks." She picked up the phone and punched the appropriate button.

"Hello, Andrew."

"Samantha. How are you?"

"Fine," she answered cautiously and braced herself for the worst. The team's owner sounded jubilant, but it must be a ploy, the calm before the tornado.

"I've been meaning to call you, but I've been up to my ears in paperwork. About this stuff in the newspaper." He paused.

Samantha swallowed hard.

Jarrett pulled up a chair, leaned forward and watched her, looking too smug. She wanted to slug him.

"I don't know exactly what you're up to," Elliott continued, "but I am *loving* it!"

Samantha's mouth dropped open in surprise. "You're what?"

"I haven't been this tickled in a dog's age. Where do you come up with these brilliant ideas?" Elliott chuckled. "You are something else. And ticket sales? Well, they took a nice jump after the story hit the streets. We've been setting records ever since. I've got to hand it to you, I never expected anything like this."

"Well, thank you," Samantha sputtered, still unable to believe what she was hearing. "I can't take all the credit."

"And you know the best part?"

Dare she ask? "No, what's that?"

"It doesn't cost me a dime." Elliott gave one of his Santa

Claus chuckles. Jarrett must have overheard, for the dimple appeared again. He had the nerve to laugh, right in front of her.

Samantha's head reeled. Elliott thought the whole thing was a joke—a publicity stunt. "I must admit, it's been something of a surprise to us, too," she offered weakly.

"Keep it up, girl. Keep it up."

"I'll see what I can do."

"Say, just out of curiosity, are you going to go out with this guy?"

"When hell freezes over," Samantha blurted out, then cringed.

Elliott chortled. "That's it! Keep 'em hanging as long as possible. Just be careful that the story doesn't get stale."

"Oh, I'm sure it won't," Samantha replied. "I hardly know *myself* what will happen next."

"Going with your gut, eh? Well, I like that. Keep up the good work."

With that, he hung up. Samantha put the handset back into the cradle. What had just happened? Instead of firing her, as she feared, Andrew Elliott had praised her. A chuckle from Jarrett brought her head swinging around. As soon as her eyes lit on him, he grinned.

"He thought it was funny, didn't he?"

"He could have fired me just as easily," she said stiffly.

"But he didn't. You should have asked for more money, a bonus for such a brilliant idea." Jarrett laced his hands across his stomach and leaned back comfortably in the chair, long legs stretched out in front of him.

His smugness acted like a shower of ice water, cooling her temper, freezing her blood. How arrogant he was! He thought he had it made, that once again he had turned the tables on her. Now he just sat there, waiting for her to fall into his arms. *Fat chance.*

"You'll notice I'm not laughing."

"Unlike you, most people do think the story is funny. Your brother was in stitches over the whole thing. In fact, he suggested a few things to tell the reporters."

"I'm sure he did." Samantha forced herself to sound tranquil and composed. She had been anything but that so far. It was time to change.

She opened a folder and pulled out the project she had been working on when Jarrett burst into the office. Picking up a pen, she began to correct the column of numbers again, completely ignoring him. She caught his frown out of the corner of her eye.

"What are you doing?"

She looked up, one eyebrow raised. "Working. I'm sure you can see yourself out. Can't you?" She turned back to her papers.

"What happens now?"

"Why, nothing." Samantha kept her tone mildly surprised while secretly reveling in his perplexed look. "Except that you leave, and I keep this business running."

"What about us?"

She laughed lightly. "Us? There *is* no us."

Jarrett's lazy, smug slouch stiffened abruptly. "But Elliott doesn't have a problem with us dating, so—" He held out his hands. "No more obstacles. We're free to see each other all we want."

Samantha sighed with just a touch of exasperation. She put her pen down, folded her hands and spoke to him as if he were seven. "Elliott may not have a problem, but I do. Jarrett, I do not want to see you or go out with you. Not now. Not ever. If you'll recall, the only time I agreed to go on a date with you was when I was tricked. There is no 'us,' nor will there ever *be* an 'us.' Now, please, I have work to do." She made a little shooing motion with her hand.

Jarrett looked dumbfounded. Samantha kept the triumph

off her face, masking it behind the tolerant irritation with which a schoolteacher might regard a naughty boy. Two could play his game. She might even play it better than he did.

"You're not serious," he said, obviously astounded.

She looked at him, straight-faced. "Of course I am."

Eyes narrowed, Jarrett studied her face for a long moment, then he stood to go. Unexpectedly, he leaned across the desk, catching her mouth in a kiss before she could protest. His tongue made a sweep of her lips, delving inside. Samantha's mouth was flooded with his delicious flavor. She couldn't protest. In some strange way, she didn't want to. His taste was like a drug for her. She was way overdue for a fix—at least fourteen long days, in fact.

As quickly as he had struck, he pulled away. Samantha sat completely still for a heartbeat, then opened her eyes. He was motionless, leaning over her desk, just inches away from her. The power in his gaze made her breath hitch.

"You're a liar," he whispered.

Her mouth dropped open to deny this, but, before she could speak, he turned and opened the door.

"See you around, Sammy," he said. He left, closing the door quietly behind him.

Samantha stared at the spot where he had just stood. Then she picked up the folder on her desk and flung it at the closed door. Paper flew through the air and began to float to the floor in lazy spirals. She could *kick* herself. Why, after fooling him so thoroughly, had she let him kiss her? And why had she enjoyed it so much? Even now, as angry as she was, she wanted him to come back and finish what he had started. His kiss had been too sudden, too hot and all too brief. She licked her tingling lips and tasted Jarrett on them.

She could also taste defeat; he had won another round, especially with that last kiss. The man was exasperating. He was so conceited and self-satisfied, as if he had just single-handedly pitched a shutout. She pushed herself out of her chair, too agitated to sit still a moment longer. She might as well expend some of her pent-up energy cleaning up the mess she had made. As she knelt on the carpet and picked up the scattered papers, Samantha continued to fume over Jarrett. *So, he thought he had cleared a path to her heart.*

"No more obstacles, my ass," she said to no one but herself.

Maybe Andrew Elliott loved the front-page headlines, but she certainly did not. She slapped the jumbled pile of documents onto her desk and sat in her chair. The pile of pink message slips glared at her again. She glared back at it. The top one was from Jim Granger of the *Times,* the most persistent of the reporters clamoring to see her. He called at least twice a day and was not above lying about his identity to get through to her.

No obstacles, indeed! Here was one right on her desk. And it was all Jarrett's doing. Suddenly an idea began to tickle the back of her brain. Since she was already in the public eye, why not use it to her advantage? Elliott was certainly for it. She had to do something to put Jarrett in his place. She would beat him at his own game. That would teach him to come strutting into her office sporting that cute, dimpled grin of his, thinking that he had conquered her by plastering her name in the papers.

She tapped the pink slip of paper against her chin, debating and scheming. The phone was in her hand in the next moment.

"*Seattle Times,*" a soft and pleasant female voice said. "How may I direct your call?"

"Jim Granger, please."

The phone clicked and a gruff, coffee-and-cigarette-stained voice answered seconds later in one clipped word: "Granger."

"Mr. Granger? This is Samantha James of Emerald Advertising." Samantha's greeting was met with silence. "I'm returning your call." More silence. "Mr. Granger? Are you there?"

"Samantha James?" he finally asked. "Really?"

"Yes, that's me." She paused. "Have I called at a bad time?"

"No. No. You caught me off guard. I thought you'd never call back." Granger was refreshingly blunt.

"Well, Mr. Granger, to be honest I hadn't planned to. But I think I *would* like my side of the story told. That is, if you think anyone's interested." Samantha could hear the cloying sweetness in her voice and bit her lip. This would be fun.

"Interested? Are you kidding? The entire city wants to know what you think of Corliss. Not to mention the rest of the country."

"Well, Jarrett—that silly boy—he hasn't been completely honest about the two of us. I don't know why. Maybe it's the reporters who are twisting his story around."

"Could be. Not all of us are honorable guys."

"Can I trust you to tell my story? In my words? Nothing more, nothing less?"

Granger didn't miss a beat. "Oh, absolutely. Ms. James, I'm one of the few reporters you can trust." There was a rustling sound. "When can we meet?"

"Well, I was hoping we might talk now. Over the phone."

"Great! I've got my questions right here all ready for you."

"Oh, you are so efficient! I like that."

"Well, then, let's jump right to the big question. What *do* you think of Jarrett Corliss?"

"Oh, I think he's a very handsome and very personable man."

"Is it true that you, and I quote, 'spurned his affections'?"

"Well, I don't think I would have used those particular words, but yes, I suppose I have done just that," Samantha agreed. "But I only did it for Jarrett's—and the team's—sake."

"How do you mean?" Granger prompted.

"Well…" Samantha paused, as if in thought. "I just don't want to interfere with his game, Jim. I can call you Jim, can't I?"

"Of course, of course," he replied. "How would you interfere with his game?"

"Oh, Jim, I couldn't live with myself if he had a losing streak because of me."

There was a puzzled silence. Samantha swung the receiver away from her mouth so the reporter wouldn't hear her smothered laughter. This *was* fun.

"Why do you think he'd lose because of you?" Granger pressed.

Samantha swung the phone back to her mouth. "Isn't it obvious? Remember the last two home games he pitched?"

"Yeah, sure. He lost both of them."

"Why do you suppose that was?" Samantha asked, deliberately leading the reporter down the path.

"Because of you?" Granger sounded skeptical.

"Jim," Samantha dropped her voice to a serious hush. "Before each of those two games, he and I spent an evening together."

"Oh? So you think that's what caused him to pitch so badly."

"What else could it be? He's usually so good. I'm just afraid our little relationship is too much distraction for him. He's such a sensitive, good-hearted man. His attention is split between me and the game, and his pitching is suffering." Samantha tried to sound sad, deeply concerned and regretful all at once.

"So you think you're jinxing his game?" Granger mused.

"I hate to admit it, especially to the whole world like this, but I know Jarrett. He's so in love and so easily distracted by it. Until I'm sure that I'm not interfering with his pitching, I can't in good conscience see him. It's too upsetting for him—for both of us."

"Oh, this is good," Granger mumbled. Samantha could hear the click of a keyboard as he typed notes. "So what would change your mind? When *would* you see him again?"

"Well, I'm not sure. I guess I would need some evidence that I'm not affecting his concentration."

Granger jumped on the train of her thoughts. "Let's say that Corliss wins the next three games he pitches. Would that show you that he's learned to concentrate?"

"Hmm. Three wins?" Samantha pretended to think it over. Really, she was calculating the odds of Jarrett winning that many games consecutively in his rotation. He had it in him if he played consistently, but so far, that had not been the case. She figured the odds at better than three to one against it but, just to be safe, she added, "Let's say five games, Jim. If he won that many, I suppose it would show he's got it together. I'd know that I'm not getting in his way, and I could safely see him again."

"Let me get this straight. He has to win the next five games he pitches?"

"Yes, every one," Samantha confirmed. She imagined Jarrett's jaw dropping when he read this in tomorrow's paper. Mr. "No-more-obstacles" was in for a big surprise.

Granger went on to ask Samantha other questions about her business, how she got her start and what it was like promoting the Rainiers. She answered cordially and thoroughly. If nothing else it was good exposure for Emerald Advertising. Why should the Rainiers get all the free publicity?

After a half hour on the phone, Granger asked his last question. Samantha hung up and sat back in her chair, a smile playing across her lips. She wished she could see Jarrett's face tomorrow when he found out what she had just done. He would get a big slap in his smug, dimpled face. Of course, he would retaliate. At the moment, that didn't concern her too much. He would have to take up her challenge. The odds were in her favor.

But a small possibility began to nag at her: what if Jarrett pulled it off and won those five games? She would be bound by her own rules to go out with him. Strange how that possibility gave her almost as much pleasure as teaching him a well-deserved lesson.

Chapter Eleven

The *Times* ran Samantha's story Friday morning. The Rainiers
were scheduled to play that day, with Jarrett as the starting
pitcher against Los Angeles. If he felt any pressure from her
dare, his pitching did not show it. He threw superbly. The
Rainiers won four to three. Clearly, Jarrett was in top form,
but this was only one game. There were four more to go.

Samantha didn't watch him pitch. She did watch the high-
lights on the late-night news. There, she saw a reporter ask
Jarrett what he thought of Samantha's challenge.

"Are you taking it seriously?"

Jarrett was solemn as a choirboy. "Of course I'm taking it
seriously. I'd do anything to win her."

There was a roar of questions from other reporters, each
vying for attention. Jarrett waved them off. "Sorry, ladies and
gents. No more questions. I've got to concentrate on my
game." He ducked away, out of sight of the cameras.

Samantha knew that the smile and wink he gave them
before he disappeared were meant for her.

As the week wore on, she made a habit of buying a paper
every morning at the newsstand near her office. Each day she
turned to the sports section first, checking the status of the
team. Five days after the first win, Jarrett pitched another

game. He won again, and Samantha felt a prickling uneasiness, which she swiftly squelched. He would start every five days in rotation, barring injuries of the team's other starting pitchers. With each start, he would advance one game closer to winning the challenge. Or he would lose.

She had not heard from him since she threw down her gauntlet. And, except for her morning ritual with the paper, she had little time to think about him or their contest. While the Rainiers were in town, Emerald Advertising was pressed to its limits. Two more commercials needed to be filmed. There were also guest appearances to coordinate. Several players—Jarrett included—were scheduled to appear on radio shows during morning and evening drive-times, answering questions about everything from baseball to their underwear size.

Pam and Carol coordinated all the radio spots while Samantha worked with Stuart and Lane on the commercials. She tried to give each team as much freedom as possible, only directing the progress when necessary. The results pleased her. As she hoped, everyone surpassed her expectations. Lane and Stuart produced two humorous, touching videos. Pam and Carol sent the ratings soaring at several radio stations with their handling of the player interviews.

The rest of Samantha's time was taken up with the influx of new business. Because of that flood, Emerald would have to add a few new people. Brenda had placed ads online and in various advertising journals. Résumés poured into the office. Brenda culled them for the best candidates and passed these on to Samantha. Now conducting interviews moved to the top of Samantha's long list of tasks.

"Who are you planning to call first?" Brenda asked, indicating the stack of résumés that sat on the corner of Samantha's desk. This was the fourth time she had asked the question that week.

Samantha eyed them wearily. "I don't know. I haven't even looked at them yet."

"Samantha, some have been here a week, and there are more coming in every day," Brenda chided.

"I haven't had time." Samantha waved her hands at her littered desk. "I promise, I'll do them today."

Brenda picked up the stack of paper. "No, I'll do them. I'll go through the pile again and put them in order, best to worst, okay?" She pinned her boss with a steely gaze. "This afternoon, you decide who to call first."

"Yes, ma'am." Samantha kept her voice meek while she bowed her head.

Brenda snorted in disbelief.

Samantha watched her very pregnant assistant move toward the door with all the grace of a drunken elephant. "Remind me again. Just how long before you desert me to have Junior?"

"Two weeks. Two blessed weeks." Brenda rolled her eyes. "Then I'll be gone for three months. And I won't even think about you or this blasted business."

"Are you sure you have to be gone that long?" Samantha cringed at the thought of having to deal with the piles of paperwork by herself. Losing Brenda was like losing a limb.

"Just don't push me." Brenda shook her finger at Samantha in warning. "I'm liable to decide to stay home with the baby and not come back until the kid graduates from medical school."

"No! Don't you dare even think of something like that, Brenda Miller. I'll drag you back by your diaper bag if I have to."

Brenda laughed and left with the stack of résumés.

Samantha wished she felt less frazzled with one stack of papers off her desk. She unearthed a file for a new client and began jotting down ideas and suggestions for Pam and Carol to work up. There was just enough time to become engrossed in the job before Debbie hailed her on the intercom speaker.

"Samantha, your brother is here. Do you have time to see him?"

No, Samantha wished she could say. Her brother picked the worst times to be a pest. She pushed the intercom button. "Sure, send him back." She jotted down the ideas still in her head and closed the file just as Boomer sauntered in the door.

"Hi, Sam. I was on my way to the stadium and decided to drop in."

Samantha laughed. "Somehow, I don't believe you. You're not the casual-caller type."

"Well, you're usually busy." Boomer grinned ruefully as though he'd been caught with his hand in the cookie jar. "But I thought I'd take a chance today. We could go to lunch."

She shook her head. "Sorry. This is one of those busy times, kiddo. Your owner has got me buried two feet under. How come you're here anyway? Isn't the team leaving for Chicago today?"

"Yeah, but we don't leave until four." He looked over the pile of work on her desk. "You do look busy, Sam. With all this work you must be raking in the dough, huh?"

"Yeah, right." Samantha snorted. "Speaking of money, when are you going to pay me back? Is that why you're here?"

Boomer dropped his large frame into the closest chair. "Well, not exactly."

"What do you mean, 'not exactly'?" Samantha surreptitiously glanced at her wristwatch. She hoped he would get to the point of his visit soon.

If Boomer noticed her impatience, he hid it well. He slouched deeper into the chair. "I have a proposition for you. Sort of an investment, now that you're a woman of means."

Samantha laughed. "I wish. I *am* getting a lot of work. But that means I'm spending more money, too."

"So, I guess you're not interested."

"Interested in what?"

"Loaning me another five thousand."

"What?" Samantha looked at Boomer sharply. "What happened to the ten thousand I just gave you?"

"You didn't just give me that, Sam. That was weeks ago."

"So what happened to it?"

"I spent it," Boomer retorted. He shifted in his chair, as if uncomfortable. "Relax. You'll get it back. It's just that I can get it to you sooner, if I get some more cash."

Samantha looked at her brother for a long moment, debating her next words. "Ray, are you in some sort of trouble?"

"No!" Boomer lunged out of his chair to pace the office. Samantha's worried gaze followed him every step of the way. "I just need something more to tide me over. I'm strapped, Samantha. You've got to help me out. I mean, things are going well for you."

Samantha chewed on her lip. She wanted to help, but she didn't like his evasiveness. "What's wrong? Isn't that ball club paying you enough these days?"

"Sure. And the team's doing great. I can already smell the bonus check. It's just that—" Boomer sat down again, his shoulders hunched. "Okay, I'll admit it. I made a bad investment and I'm out on a limb. But it's only temporary. The deal is ready to pay off next week. So I can give you your money a week from Monday."

Samantha studied him. The money was not the problem. She had reserve funds available for emergencies. Still, she didn't like the idea. "If it's a bad investment, why do you need more money to put into it?"

"It's not the investment that's bad," Boomer said impatiently. "This guy getting a divorce has screwed us all up."

"I thought you said one of the partners died."

Boomer waved a hand. "One of them is getting divorced now. It just adds to the cash flow problem." He sat forward. "If I can put another five thousand down, I can buy out my part of the deal. Someone else buys in and I get my investment back."

The convolutions of this deal made no sense to Samantha. "This sounds crazy—"

"Yeah, I know, but that's exactly how I got into the deal in the first place," he interrupted. "I should have known. If someone is getting out of such a sweet deal, it means there's something rotten underneath." Boomer sighed and rubbed a hand over his face. He seemed beaten down and tired all of a sudden. He looked at Samantha with weary eyes. "Will you lend me the money?" he asked simply.

Once more, Boomer's big plans had come to nothing. She had thought a shopping center sounded better than his previous schemes, but she had been wrong. After a long internal debate with herself, Samantha sighed.

"You'll have the money back to me soon?"

"Ten days," he vowed. "Two weeks, max."

She reached in a drawer and pulled out a checkbook. As she wrote, she laid down her rules. "This is a loan, right? Just like the first time." Samantha looked up and caught Boomer's eyes. He nodded. She scratched her name on the bottom of the check, then handed it to her brother.

"Hey, sis, thanks. Thanks a million." Boomer took the check and pressed an effusive kiss to her cheek.

"Don't let me down, Ray," Samantha said.

All smiles now, Boomer laughed. "Don't worry. You won't have any regrets. I promise."

"Good. Now scat. I've got work to do."

Boomer thanked her again and left. Samantha immediately turned her attention to the work on her desk. The morning was gone and too much remained to be done. For lunch, she ordered a turkey sandwich to be delivered from the deli on the corner. With everyone out of the office, she should be able to concentrate without interruptions. Just as she opened the paper bag, Brenda stepped into the doorway.

"Uh, Sam?"

The smell of turkey was making her mouth water and she didn't look up. "Hmm?"

"Remember what I said about having two weeks until Junior comes?"

"Yeah?" Samantha answered absently, pulling out the wrapped sandwich and a bag of chips.

"Junior's decided he doesn't want to wait that long."

The words sunk in slowly. "What?" Her head swiveled up. Brenda's face was white, and her hands clasped the base of her protruding belly. Samantha's face went white, too. "Now? You're having Junior *now?*"

Brenda nodded. Samantha leaped up from her chair. "Are you sure?"

"My water just broke," Brenda said unhappily. "Thank goodness I have one of those plastic chair mats under my desk."

Samantha's mouth dropped open in surprise, and she burst out laughing. "It'll make an interesting mess for the cleaning crew. Our bill will probably go through the roof."

Brenda laughed with her, then clamped her teeth over her bottom lip as a contraction hit. "Oh, I don't think I'm going to like this, Sam. Do I have to do it?"

Samantha smiled sympathetically and ran to put an arm around Brenda. "I think so, sweetie. You want to sit down?"

"No. They told us in Lamaze class that walking would make the contractions more bearable."

"Okay. Have you called anyone yet? Your doctor? Craig?"

"Not yet. I was so shocked when it happened. I just stood

there for a minute, then I came in here. They didn't tell me it was going to be so, so…wet!" she said plaintively.

"That's why they call it breaking water." Samantha giggled at the look of distaste on her friend's face. "How far apart are the contractions?"

"Pretty far. I've only had a couple."

"Good. Much as I love you, I'd rather not have Junior make his debut in my office." Brenda smiled, and Samantha went on, "I'm going to call your doctor first and tell him you're on your way. Then I'll call Craig. Do you want an ambulance, or will I do as a chauffeur?"

"You'll do. You're probably a lot safer to ride with than Craig would be. I just know that man is going to fall apart as soon as he knows I'm in labor. He won't be good for a thing."

Samantha and Brenda shared a fit of giggles until another contraction had Brenda gasping. Samantha supported her, rubbing her back, then went to the phone and made the calls. After she spoke to Craig, she smiled at Brenda.

"I think you're right. He's pretty much a blithering idiot just now."

"Told you," Brenda said. "I didn't marry him with my eyes closed."

Samantha grabbed her purse and ushered Brenda out the door. She refrained from announcing that they were on their way to the hospital. Samantha didn't want any delays, even ones for good wishes. As they passed the reception desk, she did tell Debbie where they were going.

"Oh, Brenda! Congratulations!"

Another contraction was gripping Brenda, and she couldn't reply. After it passed, she said, "If anyone had told me it was this much fun, I might have skipped the whole deal."

Samantha helped her out the door, down the hall and into the elevator. Leaving Brenda in the lobby of the building, she dashed across the street to get her car out of the parking lot. The hospital was north of downtown, so they zipped onto the freeway, through light, midday traffic. She held Brenda's hand as the contractions came closer and closer together.

"This kid seems to be in a hurry," she commented.

"Good," Brenda replied. "It couldn't happen too quickly for me."

Brenda's obstetrician met them in the emergency room and helped her through admitting. A birthing room was prepared, and Brenda was quickly ensconced in the peaceful surroundings. Craig arrived, flushed and flustered. Samantha left the two alone together after sharing a private smile with Brenda. She volunteered to retrieve Brenda's suitcase from their house and come back to see how things were going.

Six and a half hours later, Brenda delivered a beautiful baby girl into the hands of her ecstatic father. Less than an hour later, Samantha held the new baby and spoke to a proud but exhausted Brenda.

"Don't think just because she's adorable, that I'm going to let you off work for longer than three months."

Brenda took her new daughter from Samantha and gazed down at the wrinkled little face. "I don't know, Sam. Maybe this would be a good time to ask for that raise you keep promising me."

Samantha laughed.

SAMANTHA WALTZED THROUGH the office first thing the next morning and stuck pink bubble-gum cigars in everyone's mouths. She announced that Brenda had had a girl and both mother and daughter were doing well. She was so proud and happy, she could have been mistaken for one of the baby's parents. Her festive mood permeated the entire office, and spirits were high. Samantha's mood dipped when she turned to the sports page and found that Jarrett had won another game against Chicago. Three wins. He was past the halfway mark. It couldn't last, she told herself. So what if he had won three games in a row? He was bound to lose the next one. Or at least the fifth game.

The Rainiers were on an extended road trip. After Chicago, they flew to Texas. Jarrett would pitch the fourth game of his five-game challenge there. Samantha finally gave in to her need to see him in action. She slipped away from work early one afternoon. At five-thirty, she was in front of her television watching every pitch.

From the first inning, Jarrett made his job look easy. Tonight, his fastballs were particularly effective. Several hitters could only shake their head as the ball whizzed past them before they could swing at it. But when the camera focused in on Jarrett's face, Samantha could see the strain in his blue eyes. Then in the seventh inning it happened.

The Rainiers were on top, two to zero. Excitement built with every batter struck out. Would this be a shutout? Would Jarrett and the Rainiers keep their opponents from making a single run? The camera zoomed in again to frame Jarrett. His eyes were locked on the next batter he faced. He nodded at his catcher's signal, then wound up for the throw. The camera panned back. Samantha chewed her lip, her nerves stretched taut.

The ball that should have winged its way safely into the catcher's mitt took a wrong turn. At the last moment it swerved close to the batter—dangerously close. Traveling at close to ninety-five miles an hour, it was transformed from a baseball into a bullet. The batter spun away, avoiding the missile as it flew past him. In the next second, he rushed forward, ready to hit Jarrett in return for the wild, dangerous pitch. The camera closed in swiftly on the batter's box, catching the angry toss of the bat, and the helmet flung with equal vehemence. The catcher ran up, and the home plate umpire stepped forward to avert disaster.

Then the camera swiveled back to the pitcher's mound. Samantha gasped when she saw Jarrett hunched over, nursing his shoulder and grimacing in pain. The batter stopped his headlong rush, confused. The catcher and the umpire were riveted in place, too. Coaches and trainers swarmed past them to the mound and enshrouded Jarrett. Seconds later they escorted him to the dugout and out of sight. What had happened?

The announcers made speculations about Jarrett's history and probable future. Every detail of his past injuries was dragged out for examination. Samantha sat on the edge of her seat. The waiting was agony. Play on the field resumed almost immediately when Rosenthal stepped up the mound to take Jarrett's place. Samantha paid little attention to the game, though the relief pitcher held the lead, only giving up one run. The Rainiers won, two to one.

Samantha waited and waited for an announcement about Jarrett. She sat through every interview and ounce of speculation of the post-game show. She avidly searched the screen for glimpses of him when players were interviewed in the locker room after the game. Finally he appeared surrounded by reporters.

"Jarrett, what happened out there?"

Jarrett shrugged, holding both ends of a towel around his neck. "Just got a little distracted, I guess." His smile was easy. "I've got a lot riding on these games you know," he added with a wink.

"You were holding your shoulder," one man called out. "Did you hurt it?"

"Does this mean you're going to take a rest from pitching?" another interrupted.

"Are you going to have to have surgery again?"

"What about—"

Jarrett held a hand up. "Wait a minute, now. Y'all are jumping the gun here. My shoulder's just fine. This was a tough game against a good team, and pitching a shutout is hard work."

"So you're going back on the mound?"

"I've got another game to win, a few days from now," Jarrett answered with a sly grin. "Y'all know it's an important one."

"Because of Samantha James?"

Jarrett's expression was serious, but his eyes were filled with glee. "Because we're playing Kansas City," he corrected the reporter.

Samantha laughed along with the journalists. Part of her laughter came from relief. If Jarrett was joking with these reporters he couldn't be hurting too much, could he? Moments later, Jarrett ducked out of sight and the reports turned to another player. Samantha flicked off the television and tossed the remote onto the coffee table.

Stretching, she rose and walked out onto her balcony. A ferry, brightly lit against black water, glided from Seattle to Bainbridge Island. Samantha followed it with her eyes as she considered the outcome of the evening's game. Jarrett had won. One more win, and she would have no choice but to go out with him. Anxiety plucked at her. *Only one more game.*

Samantha closed her eyes and drew in the night air. The afterimage of the ferry lights sparkled behind her closed lids. When she opened her eyes, she admitted the truth to herself: she wanted Jarrett to win. Even if he was an arrogant jock, she wanted to explore the passion between them that burned so hotly. A breeze lofted across her skin, and Samantha shivered.

Would he pull it off? Regardless of his jokes during the post-game interview, he had hurt himself tonight. Because of her, he was pushing himself. Perhaps too far. Regret warred with the anxiety in her heart. The last thing she wanted was for Jarrett to ruin his career for her. But she could not stop the contest now. Even if she issued a retraction, Jarrett would not let her pull the prize away when he was so close to seizing it.

The bargain was struck. No injured shoulder and no regrets would change the terms now. Jarrett would come home and pitch. She would be in the stands cheering him on. If he won, she would give him his reward.

And if he lost?

For that possibility, she had no answer.

Chapter Twelve

Sicks Stadium was packed to capacity for the third game of the series against Kansas City. The Rainiers had narrowly lost the first game. The local fans were boisterous this evening, craving a win for their team. The completion of Jarrett's challenge only added to the furor. Samantha stopped just beyond the stadium's entrance, letting the roar of the crowd wash over her. The eager shouts, the smell of popcorn and peanuts and the festive march of the organ music all melded to a perfect reflection of how she felt inside.

Her heart sped with excitement, sweeping her up into the enthusiasm and joy of the moment. Tonight she would join in cheering Jarrett and the Rainiers to victory. She had commandeered one of the two seasons tickets Emerald Advertising had been given at the beginning of their contract. Usually the pair of tickets rotated among the employees, so everyone had a chance to root for the home team. Though not much of a perk at the time, now the tickets were highly prized.

Samantha wove through the crowds to the VIP section. She had been hoping to slip unnoticed into her seat, but she was immediately thwarted. Heads turned as she came down the aisle, as if people had waited expectantly for her entrance. Some pointed. Others whistled. She heard her name and

Jarrett's mentioned in the same breath by those nearby. As much as she wished for anonymity, the attention was unsurprising. Her picture had accompanied Jarrett's in all the local papers and a few national ones as well.

Samantha sat and flipped through the pages of her program. She tried to ignore the stares and comments, but she felt like a solitary fish in a very large fishbowl. Every direction she turned, eyes gawked at her. Cameras televising the game zoomed in and her face was flashed on every screen in the stadium.

The players took the field and, thankfully, attention shifted to the game. Samantha breathed a sigh of relief. As eagerly as the rest of the crowd, she scanned the field. Boomer was in left field. She didn't see Jarrett at first, then caught a glimpse of him warming up in the bullpen. Would he see that she was here, waiting and watching? Anticipation grew to an almost unbearable level. She was one game—nine short innings—away from being in Jarrett's arms.

A figure stepped in front of her, blocking her view, and Samantha looked up. It was Lane, taking the seat next to her.

"Whew!" he exclaimed. "I thought I'd never make it. Traffic was hideous—like a pack of slugs out for a Sunday slime."

"You went home after work?"

"Yeah, what a mistake. All these people, just to watch eighteen guys chase a little ball. Who'd have thunk it?"

She smiled at his dramatics. Earlier in the day, Lane and Pam had flipped a coin for the extra ticket. Samantha was glad he had won the toss. He would be a good, lighthearted companion for this most important game. He and Stuart usually took the pair of tickets together, since Lane's girlfriend hated baseball. Lane loved the game and he knew how to have fun, win or lose, until the last inning. For this game, Samantha would follow the same rules. Tonight there were no details to manage, no business to tend. She would sit back and try to watch the game like any other fan.

The crowd stood for the national anthem. Jarrett took the mound, and Samantha's heart seemed to stop. He took several easy warm-up throws. The umpire cried, "Play ball!" The game had begun.

Jarrett stood in the center of the field, sizing up his first opponent, poised and confident. He seemed unaware of the excited crowd as he rubbed the ball, finding a grip on the leather and stitching. The thought that those same strong hands had touched her body—and might do so again—thrilled Samantha beyond comprehension.

Jarrett wound up, threw the ball. Strike one. As Samantha watched him, she looked for any signs of injury left over from the game a few nights ago. But Jarrett pitched with the same skill, speed and control as he had most of the season. Occasionally, he rotated his shoulder gingerly, as if testing it, but Samantha couldn't tell if he was in pain or just being cautious. At the end of the fifth inning, the score was one to nothing, the Rainiers on top. Jarrett had not allowed a single hit. By the sixth, the score was unchanged. Jarrett was pitching a perfect game.

At the top of the seventh inning, Jarrett had struck out his first batter when it happened again. It was a strange repetition of the game Samantha had watched on television. Jarrett's second pitch went wild, careening past the batter, into the mesh protecting the fans behind home plate. Jarrett tore off his glove, grabbing for his shoulder. He grimaced in pain while Samantha's nails bit into her palms.

The tumultuous crowd hushed as the coach, two trainers and the catcher rushed out to the mound. Samantha leaned forward in her seat, as if by doing so she could hear what they said. A trainer was moving Jarrett's arm in strange contortions. As the coach was talking to him, Jarrett shook his head fiercely. The trainer spoke, grim-faced. The coach replied, and Jarrett's expression hardened. Action paused for agonizing moments, then a decision was made. Jarrett stayed on the mound, and the other men went back to their places. Samantha sat back, unsure whether to be relieved or angry that Jarrett stayed in the game. He was pushing himself too far.

The rest of the inning, Jarrett's throws were less controlled, less certain. He walked two batters before striking out a third. The next man hit a pop fly that was snagged by Boomer for an easy out. The crowd rose to give Jarrett a standing ovation as he walked off the field. Samantha stood with them, then remained on her feet to sing "Take Me Out to the Ball Game" during the seventh inning stretch. Just standing was a welcome change after sitting on the edge of her seat, watching Jarrett pitch to complete the inning. She was tempted to go down to the locker room to ask someone about him. She stayed to watch the game instead. Jarrett had walked off the field under his own power, so he must be all right.

Kansas City switched to their relief pitcher in the bottom of the seventh. The Rainiers' designated hitter got a single that put Alvendia on second. Boomer made good on his name and socked one to center field. Alvendia risked it and raced for home plate. After the dust cleared, the umpire made his call. Safe. The Rainiers led by two. They were kept from scoring for the rest of the inning and the teams rotated, bringing them to the top of the eighth.

"Oh my God!" Lane exclaimed excitedly. "What is he doing back out there?"

Samantha's mouth dropped open as she looked over where Lane was pointing. Jarrett was taking the mound once more. Deafening hoots and applause greeted his appearance, echoing the sudden pounding of Samantha's heart.

"He's lost his mind," she breathed.

"How did he convince the coach to keep him on the mound?" Lane darted a glance at Samantha.

She knew immediately what he was thinking, along with everyone else in the stadium: she was the reason Jarrett had returned to the mound. Samantha clenched her jaw, fighting back the urge to scream. How could he risk himself this way? She knew the answer to that question, though. Jarrett wanted this game—win or lose—all for himself. He would let no relief pitcher earn the prize for him. Samantha was torn between laughter and tears. Honored that he would fight so hard for her, she could have strangled him for his pigheaded stubbornness.

As the gigantic stadium screens broadcasted her image to the thousands of fans, Samantha held her emotions in check. She watched her own face to be sure it was as neutral as she could manage, amazed that the whirl of feeling inside her was so easily hidden. She owed it to Jarrett to remain calm, at least on the outside. She would not let her fears for him affect his playing.

Jarrett pitched another perfect inning, but Kansas City still had a chance at the top of the ninth. Again, Jarrett walked to the mound. That urge to scream out her fear and frustration surged in her throat once more. Jarrett was taking too many risks.

He struck the first batter out effortlessly. The second was not so easy. Jarrett had lost his rhythm. Some pitches were deadly accurate. Some were wild. He threw five times, three balls and two strikes. His sixth flew low and outside. The fans booed as the umpire called a fourth ball. Kansas City now had a man on first. The next batter was worse. He seemed to catch Jarrett's fastball just in time. Three times he hit a foul. Luckily, he did it a fourth time and fouled out.

With two outs and victory in sight, bedlam broke loose in the stands. Jarrett seemed just as unaware of it as he had since the start. He took his time appraising the player in the batter's box, one of the best hitters in the division. Although Jarrett's pitching had deteriorated rapidly over the last two innings, he still looked unperturbed. If anything, the yelling from the stands seemed to relax him.

Two fastballs, pure blinding speed, each followed by two swings, both misses. The crowd was on its feet. The next pitch was obviously a ball, high and outside. Everyone in the stadium groaned in agony. The next pitch went to the same place. Carefully, Jarrett prepared for the next pitch. He rubbed his sore shoulder and took two deep breaths. The whole stadium seemed to breathe with him. He wound up and unleashed another pitch. Time slowed as the ball curled out of Jarrett's hand into the air, flying over dirt and grass to the plate. The batter swung, controlled muscle and sinew. The stadium was silent as the ball landed with a resounding smack in the catcher's mitt.

Jarrett had done it. He had won.

Samantha rose to her feet, arms in the air, unable to contain her shout of pure joy. Her paean was lost in the cheers of the people around her. Tears filled her eyes, and she threw her arms around Lane. He danced a victory jig and yelled something in her ear that was lost in the deafening roar. Then he hauled her up on her seat so they could see over the heads of the crowd. Samantha could see the team engulf Jarrett in a mass of exuberance.

As she stood on her toes to see him, Jarrett swung his head around to where she was standing. She was sure there was no way he could see her, but he pulled off his cap and waved it anyway, a broad grin on his face. His waving seemed to charge the people around her. They began yelling and applauding in her direction. Several called out to her, insisting that she join Jarrett on the field. Samantha wasn't sure what they had in

mind, but she soon found out. An impatient bunch of fans
mobbed her. "Okay, lady, up you go," one of them yelled. With
much laughing and cheering, she was lifted from her seat
above a mass of people and carried to the field.

It was useless to struggle against the crowd's will. The fans
wanted her on the field with Jarrett. Since there were many
more of them than of her, she didn't resist. Lane joined in the
frenzy, and led the way from the stands. Once on the field,
Samantha was carried to the crowd of players. The two masses
of shifting bodies collided. Samantha found herself safe in
Jarrett's arms surrounded by the happy chaos.

JARRETT SWEPT SAMANTHA INTO his embrace, pressing her to
his full length. She felt so good. He buried his face in her neck
and inhaled the warm fragrance of her soft body. He ached to
hold her more intimately, without all the fetters of clothing
between them. He wanted to carry her off to a private corner
of the stadium where they could be alone without all these
prying eyes. As the crowd was not about to let them escape
and since Jarrett could not wait, he kissed her instead. It was
a long, passionate kiss. It produced raucous cheers and
catcalls around them, while flashbulbs burst like fireworks.

Samantha had a dazed, soft look on her face when he lifted
his head from her lush mouth. Then she went red with embarrassment as she realized that all the cheers were for them.
Jarrett gazed at her in triumph. She was *his!* The look on her
face assured him that she accepted that fact, even relished it.

After the kiss and more photos, the other players and uniformed officers guided them to the locker room. Just before
entering the corridor, a reporter elbowed his way in front of
them and thrust his microphone in their faces.

"So what happens now?" he shouted over the echoing noise
of the celebration. "Where will you go on your first date?"

Jarrett kept Samantha glued tightly to his side and answered, "I think we'll keep that much a secret."

Other reporters saw the pair and ran over to ask their questions, everything from when the date would happen to how many children they planned on having. Jarrett answered most of the questions, but Samantha managed to trade a few quips with the reporters. As fast as they could ask a question, she had an answer for it. But he could tell the experience was overwhelming for her. Finally, Jarrett decided that the reporters had gotten enough. He pulled her off to one side, ignoring the questions that still flew at them.

"Go home. I'll see you there as soon as I can." His lips were close to her ear and he couldn't resist reaching out with his tongue, tracing the delicate edge. She shivered, but didn't pull away.

"Good idea," she agreed. "But how am I going to get out of here in one piece?"

Jarrett glanced around quickly and found the person he needed. He pulled her close once more and elbowed his way past reporters and teammates, apologizing as they squeezed through. He grabbed Peter Brinks and spoke his request into his ear. With a nod, Peter took Samantha's arm and led her toward a door marked Employees Only.

Just before she passed through the door, Samantha turned for a last look at Jarrett. He smiled and waved, mouthing the word *later,* before plunging into the crowd and threading his way to the locker room. Security started herding people off the field before they could stop Jarrett with more questions. He slipped into the locker room unhindered and joined his teammates in celebration.

AT THE FIRST KNOCK, Samantha bolted down the hall to open the door. The wild beating of her heart only intensified when she saw Jarrett filling the doorway. He was looking at her so intently, desire—mixed with tenderness and need—in his clear blue gaze. No one had ever looked at her like this before. He took her breath away.

"I forgot to congratulate you—" she managed to say, but the words were cut off as Jarrett reached for her and hauled her into his arms, kicking the door shut behind him. His mouth unerringly found hers and drew her into his heat and passion. As during their kiss on the field, Samantha was lost. Time and place deserted her. She only knew that she was where she belonged—in Jarrett's arms.

Slowly, he deepened the kiss, wordlessly begging for entrance to her mouth. As she once more tasted his unique flavor, Samantha realized she had been starved for Jarrett. His mouth left hers to travel over her face, strewing kisses on her eyes, nose and cheeks. Eagerly, she returned the caresses, drowning in the luxury of being able to touch him. Finally, he buried his face in the curve of her neck and held her to him, close and tight.

"I missed you, darlin'," he said. "So much. *Too* much."

"I missed you, too, Jarrett." A sigh of pure contentment flowed through her lips.

After a long moment, Jarrett pulled back to cup Samantha's face between his hands. His eyes searched hers. "I did what you wanted, Sammy, didn't I? Five games."

Tears welled up in Samantha's eyes. "Yes, Jarrett. You did everything I asked and more. I'm sorry—"

Jarrett stopped her words with another quick, hard kiss. "No. There's nothing to be sorry about."

"But your shoulder—"

"Will be just fine."

"But—"

"No, Samantha." His kiss was longer this time, with a tenderness that sent her tears overflowing. He wiped them away with his thumbs. "That's behind us. We're together now. That's all that matters."

Samantha slid her arms up around his neck, drawing him close. "Yes," she agreed. "We are together."

In one smooth sweep, he picked her up and carried her to the bedroom, gently placing her in the middle of her bed. Then he joined her, aligning his long length with hers. The time for words was past. Samantha kissed him tenderly. With hands and mouths touching each other, she spoke all the things in her heart. Exultation and ecstasy, love and longing, all in murmurs of inarticulate pleasure.

Slowly, relishing each inch, Jarrett's hands traveled over her from shoulder to hips, baring her skin to his touch as he went. At the first touch of his mouth on her breast, a sigh and a whimper rose in the back of Samantha's throat. Her fingers paused their eager dance down the buttons of his shirt as he licked, then gently bit her tender flesh. A moan came from her lips when he pulled first one, then the other nipple into his mouth. Her skin flushed in pleasure from his adorations.

All at once, she needed to feel all of his skin against hers. She reached for the last of his buttons as Jarrett kissed her mouth. His tongue laved hers, exploring and teasing. Samantha pushed the shirt from his broad shoulders. Running her hands over his muscled back to his shoulders, she felt the ridge of scar tissue. She drew back, searching his eyes, trying to see into him.

"Does it hurt?" she asked, tracing the imperfection delicately with her fingers.

Jarrett smiled and ran a trail of moist kisses down her neck to her shoulder. "Only when I throw a baseball."

Samantha refused to be detoured. "Tell me the truth."

"The truth?" Jarrett raised his head and looked at her for

a long moment. His face grew serious. "The truth is, I wasn't sure if I could make it past the sixth inning tonight. About the seventh, I got scared. But I kept thinking of you up in the stands watching me. I wasn't about to quit."

"I was scared in the seventh, too," Samantha said softly. "You shouldn't have stayed in the game, Jarrett."

"I had to, Sammy. I needed to win. I needed—need—you."

Samantha was humbled by his words. Never before had anyone made such a sacrifice, risked so much for her. "I need you, too. I'm sorry I ever denied it."

Her words seemed to set off a fire in Jarrett. Rolling onto his back, he pulled her over him and rained kisses on her wherever he could reach. His hands excited her with every stroke as her clothes disappeared under his questing caresses. Samantha caressed him in turn, running her hands down the hard muscles of his chest. When she teased his tight, flat nipples through the crisp curls of chest hair, his groan brought a low laugh from her. As her hands slipped lower to the buttons on the faded blue jeans he wore, his breath seemed to stop.

Samantha ran a finger down the placket of buttons that held the soft denim closed. Feeling the hard, pulsating flesh beneath, she marveled at how the buttons held against the pressure. Slowly, prolonging the pleasure and agony for them both, she eased each one open. Jarrett's hips writhed against her as her fingers brushed him. His breath was harsh now, his muscles tight. When her hand slipped past the denim and she took him into her hands, enclosing him in a gentle embrace, he groaned again.

"Darlin', you're killin' me."

Samantha laughed softly. "After all you've been through? I doubt it." She soothed the hot, hard skin, which only seemed to inflame him more.

"I never thought you were a tease," he gasped.

"I'm not. I just enjoy playing a little game now and then."
She paused and stroked a fingertip against the sensitive under-
side of his shaft. "You like games, don't you?"

Jarrett laughed and moaned at the same time. "*Like* is not
quite the right word."

She laughed again as he rolled her on to her back, kicking
off his jeans as he did so. "Let's see how you like it."

In seconds, Samantha was writhing and moaning. Everywhere he touched sent shivers of pleasure throughout her
body, short-circuiting her brain. All she could see, feel, taste
was Jarrett. She was helpless beneath his hands and loving
every minute of it.

Finally, when they were both at the edge of control, Jarrett
slipped away from her for a moment to pull a condom out of
his jeans pocket and protect them both. Seconds later, he came
between her legs and thrust himself into her in one long glide.
Staring deeply into her eyes, he rocked into her, taking them
closer and closer to the final fire. All her love shone from her
eyes. She could see the same in his gaze, too. She wrapped her
legs around his waist and clutched him to her. Pleasure such
as she had never felt washed through her as, with one final
thrust of his hips, Jarrett pushed them both into the flames.

Afterward, hearts thundering, they lay wrapped in each
other's arms. Samantha had never felt so content, so full of
life. Jarrett's fingers lazily stroked up and down her arm. She
cuddled into his embrace, her head resting on his shoulder.
Slowly, her heart returned to a steady beat, but it somehow
felt lighter. She turned her head to look at him.

"So, Mr. Corliss, when do you collect your prize?"

"My prize?" Jarrett sighed and reached out to catch her lips
with his, his eyes still closed. "What do you mean?"

"Your first date with me."

He rose up on one elbow to smile down at her. "Our *first*

date, Sammy? I seem to remember taking you out for an Italian dinner."

She laughed. "Well, technically, it will be our second date. But it *is* the first one we've both agreed on."

Jarrett brushed a finger over her lips, then dropped a kiss on the end of her nose. "Tomorrow night. I'll pick you up at seven o'clock. Wear something romantic."

"Okay. Where are we going?"

"It's a surprise." His smile was secretive, piquing her interest.

Samantha tugged at the hand that had come up to tickle the sensitive skin at her throat. "But what if I'm disappointed?"

Jarrett laughed. "You won't be. Trust me."

She knew, by the look on his face, that he wouldn't tell her any more. "All right, but I hate surprises."

He leaned over and lightly kissed her lips. "You'll love this one."

When he turned her in his arms and began to blaze a burning path down her throat to her breast, Samantha's attention shattered. Future surprises were forgotten in the wonder of their passion for one another.

Chapter Thirteen

Samantha beat her employees out of the office, walking out the door at five o'clock on the dot. She jumped into her car and wound her way through the busy streets toward home, praying for no traffic jams on the West Seattle Bridge. As she drove, she wondered what Jarrett had up his sleeve for tonight's surprise.

Inside her condo, she put on music and danced as she prepared for her first *real* date with Jarrett. This time there would be no worries, no regrets afterward. She was excited, nervous and happy all at once. Digging through her closet, Samantha looked at, then rejected, several dresses. None fit Jarrett's requirement of "romantic." Finally, behind several other outfits, she found the perfect dress, one she had never worn. Sea-green chiffon with a full skirt, spaghetti straps, and deeply scooped back, the dress was ultrafeminine. She had bought it because she couldn't resist the beautiful fabric and the way it made her feel. It was a dress to wear for someone special, but no one had ever fit that role. Not until tonight.

She laid it across the bed in a froth of green, then chose lingerie to wear beneath it for another romantic surprise. High-heeled, strappy white sandals completed her choice. With her outfit chosen, Samantha wound her hair on top of her head for a quick shower. That finished, she applied a light layer of makeup: powder, blush, eye shadow, liner to highlight her eyes, mascara, and she was done. She slipped into the dress and twirled in front of the mirror. Jarrett's eyes were going to drop right out of his head. As she unpinned her hair and brushed it thoroughly, the phone rang. Samantha smiled, knowing who was on the other end of the line.

She grabbed the handset. "Hey, lover-boy. Are you ready for me?"

"Uh, is this Samantha?"

"Jarrett?"

"No, Sam. It's Boomer."

"Boomer." Samantha felt a deep blush spread over her face. "I thought you were Jarrett. We have a date tonight."

"Yeah, I know." He sounded subdued.

Samantha sat down on the edge of the bed with a stifled sigh and glanced at the clock. She only had a half hour to spare before Jarrett arrived.

"What's wrong?"

"I need your help."

Of course you do. "Can it wait, Ray? Jarrett's on his way and—"

"I'm in jail, Sam."

"What?" Her heart threatened to leap out of her chest. "In jail? What are you doing in jail?"

"I got arrested." Boomer sounded irritated, then sighed harshly. There was a pause. "Listen, I can't talk too long. Can you come bail me out?"

"Why were you arrested, Ray?" Samantha's mind was spinning around, unable to wrap itself around the idea of her brother in jail.

"Gambling."

"What? What kind of gambling?"

"What *kind* of gambling, Sam? The *illegal* kind," Boomer nearly shouted. "It wasn't bingo, that's for damn sure. Please, Sam, you've gotta come and get me out."

"Okay, okay, I'm on my way."

"Thanks." His voice sounded relieved.

"Do you have a lawyer?" Samantha asked quickly, sensing he was about to hang up.

"No. Can you get one?"

"Yes…well, I'll—I'll see what I can do. Just sit tight, I'll be there as soon as I can."

"I'm not going anywhere." There was a click and then dead air.

Samantha stared at the phone in her hand for a long minute, then hung up. Her brother in jail? It made no sense. She sat for a moment, picturing him in a cell. At the end of the call, Boomer had sounded very young—young and frightened. The thought disturbed her, almost as much as the worry about what he'd done wrong.

She dialed Brenda first. Craig was a lawyer and, even if he couldn't help, he might know another attorney who could.

Brenda answered. "Hello?"

"Brenda, it's me, Samantha."

"Hey. It's good to hear from you."

"How's Katie?" Samantha tried to keep her voice cheerful.

"She's great. She's just finishing her before-dinner snack," Brenda replied with a chuckle.

"Bren, I need to talk to Craig. Is he there or is he still at work?" Samantha couldn't keep her voice from shaking.

Brenda must have heard it. "What's wrong?"

"I just got a call from Ray. He's in jail. He needs a lawyer. I was hoping Craig could help."

"What? In jail? Jeez, Sam, that's terrible. Craig's here. Hang on, I'll get him."

Craig came on the line and Samantha told him what little she knew. "What do I do?"

"First, if possible, we bail him out. I'll meet you down at the courthouse as soon as I can get there." His calm, matter-of-fact voice steadied Samantha.

She hung up the phone, dashed out of the bedroom and snatched up her purse. As she did so, she remembered her date with Jarrett. She dialed his number on the way to her car. No answer. She left a brief message, explaining what had happened and told him she would call him later.

Samantha fought her way back through rush-hour traffic to the courthouse. Since it was after hours, parking downtown was not too much of a problem. She found a spot and ran across the street to a boxy, institutional-gray building. Craig had not yet arrived when she got inside. Too agitated to sit, Samantha paced the corridor, waiting amid an amazing array of people.

Even at seven-thirty in the evening, the courthouse bustled with activity. Who would have thought there was so much legal business conducted at this late hour? A policeman escorted a man in handcuffs past her, both men stoic. Samantha swallowed hard, picturing Boomer in the same predicament. Would she see him in handcuffs soon? Or behind bars? Her name was called, and she gratefully turned to see Craig striding across the lobby in her direction. He was a tall, handsome man dressed in an immaculate gray-pinstripe suit, red tie and crisp white shirt. She greeted him with a hug.

"Samantha. It's good to see you."

She laughed a little. "Even though I'm ruining your evening?"

"At least you got me out of changing a diaper," he joked. "Brenda said to tell you thanks for nothing."

"How are the new mother and baby?"

"They're getting along fine. Brenda says you should come by more often. Of course, since we've been reading about you so regularly in the papers, she figured you were busy with other things." He grinned knowingly in the same way that many people had recently.

"I'll come over soon and give you all the details. Shall we get *this* little detail out of the way first?"

Craig nodded and went straight to the matter at hand. "I'll go see what the charge is exactly and when Ray will be arraigned. Then we can get the wheels turning. It'll be a couple of hours, I assume, but I'll see what I can do to hurry things along." Craig patted her on the arm and disappeared into the chaos of the courtrooms.

After he left, Samantha found a seat and once more watched the activity whirl around her. Time seemed to grind to a halt. She looked down at the dress she wore and smiled mirthlessly. *Some romantic evening.* She flipped her phone open, but there were no calls, so she slipped it back into her purse. She wished Jarrett would call, but she didn't want to call him again. She didn't think he would say, "I told you so," but his already low opinion of Boomer would hit rock bottom now.

"Samantha!"

She looked up at the sound of her name and saw Jarrett striding toward her. He was dressed formally in a charcoal suit, a paisley-blue tie knotted at his neck. Heads turned as he passed, not only because he was famous, but because he was so handsome. A wash of relief swept through her. She stood and slipped past the few people separating them and was immediately enveloped in his embrace. It was all she could do to not burst into tears. Instead, she clung to him tightly, taking comfort from his strong arms.

"What happened?" he asked, pulling back just enough to see her face. "Boomer was arrested?"

"That's all I know." Samantha took a deep breath, trying to control her shaking voice. Now that Jarrett was here, her calm had deserted her. "He said it was because of gambling, but I don't know anything else. Craig—Brenda's husband—is here somewhere."

As she spoke, Craig appeared from the end of the hall. Samantha introduced him to Jarrett. The two men shook hands.

"What's going on, Craig?" Samantha asked anxiously.

"Ray's been arraigned and now we have to post bond. Do you have your checkbook with you?"

Samantha wrote the check he requested without another thought.

"It shouldn't be long now," Craig reassured her. "Just the formalities to get through. I'll be back with Ray in a little while." He disappeared again, and the wait continued.

Jarrett and Samantha sat on a bench holding hands. "I'm sorry about our date."

He squeezed her hand. "Don't worry about that, Sammy. Your brother is more important than our dinner."

Samantha closed her eyes tightly. "I can't believe this is happening," she whispered. "I didn't think Ray would do something like this."

Before he could reply, a disturbance at the back of the hall caught their attention. Samantha saw what looked like several cameras and people with microphones talking with a uniformed man. Then they all looked in her direction and, as they did, Boomer came through the other door with Craig by his side. The group of reporters rushed forward with cameramen tailing close behind.

"Boomer, why'd they arrest you?" one of them called, nearly spearing him with a microphone.

Boomer looked at the cameras and then at Samantha, panic showing in his eyes. Samantha and Jarrett hastened to his side.

Craig answered the woman's question. "My client has no comment at this point."

"Is it true he was arrested for gambling?"

"The charges are a matter of public record. I'm sure you can read them as well as I can. All I will say is that my client and I are confident that the truth will be revealed in the due process of law."

"But—"

"No comment," Craig replied firmly. He gripped one of Boomer's arms, and Samantha took the other. They edged past the cameras and hurried to the doors. Boomer had not said a word. Then the reporters pointed their microphones at Jarrett.

"What about you, Jarrett? Were you arrested, too?"

"No!" Samantha answered, appalled at the question. In that instant, she saw what a mistake it had been for Jarrett to join her at the courthouse. Now the reporters had *two* Rainiers to write about in conjunction with the arrest.

"I'm just here for Samantha," Jarrett answered, unperturbed. Then he added, "Y'all will have to excuse us."

While Jarrett diverted the reporters' attention, Craig drew Samantha down the hallway. "Take Ray home with you and don't answer the phone." He looked back at the reporters. "This is going to make the late news. I recommend that Ray contact team management as soon as possible. Whenever they want to see him, I think it would be best if I went along to advise him of his legal rights."

Boomer nodded his head dumbly. He was in a daze and barely seemed to register the words. Samantha wanted to shake him. Now, after her fright had died away, anger came roaring in to take its place.

"I'll call Andrew Elliott as soon as we get home. He'll probably want to see us right away."

"Good. Call me later. Here's where you can reach me at the office, tomorrow, too." Craig handed her a card with his business and mobile phone numbers.

"Thanks, Craig. I appreciate your help."

Jarrett caught up with them, closely followed by the pack of reporters. "I'll meet you at your place."

"I don't think you should be involved in this, Jarrett. It's bad enough that Ray—"

"Too late," Jarrett interrupted her protest with a light kiss. "Take Ray home, Sammy. I'll be there as soon as I can shake these guys."

He held the door for Samantha as he and Craig blocked the reporters from following her and Boomer. Samantha could hear their shouted questions as she led Boomer to her car. The drive home was completed in silence, the tension between them palpable. Samantha was ready to explode in anger at her younger brother. Once safely in the condo, she let loose.

"What happened, Ray? Why did they arrest you?"

"I told you, Sam. Gambling."

"There's more to it than that. I want the whole story. Don't leave anything out."

Boomer sat on the sofa, slouching down in defeat. "I thought I could win it all back, I really did."

"Win what back?"

"The money you lent me—"

"You gambled with the money I lent you?" Samantha was appalled. "Why, Ray?"

"I had to, Sam. The deal went sour."

"That deal that got tied up because one of the partners died?" Boomer nodded. "He wasn't the only thing that died."

"What do you mean?" Samantha asked. She sat down facing him, eyes intent on his face.

"The deal fell through."

"Explain this to me, Ray. What has all this got to do with you borrowing money to gamble? Start at the beginning."

Boomer rubbed a hand over his face, pressing thumb and

forefinger against his eyes. When he began, his voice was soft, his eyes on the carpet at his feet. "About six months ago, I heard from a broker that there was a piece of land that was being considered for a shopping center. He told me that he knew this development company was going to go for this particular parcel. So we talked to the owner and offered to option the property. I thought I could turn around and sell the option to the developer and make a quick profit."

Samantha looked at him. This was a side to her brother that she hadn't seen before. If asked, she would have laughed at the idea that Boomer James thought of anything other than baseball and women. He caught her look of disbelief.

"I'd done it before, Sam. It works!"

"But not this time?"

"No," he said softly. "The developer got a better deal on a parcel across the street. I didn't have the money to perform on the option, so I lost everything I'd put down."

"How much?" Samantha whispered.

"A lot."

"How much, Ray?"

"You don't want to know."

"Yes, I do," she hissed. "Tell me. Now."

"About five hundred thousand."

Samantha swallowed. The number was higher than she had suspected. "Five hundred thousand dollars? How could you lose so much?"

"It was a pay-as-you-go deal. I kept making option payments because I thought it was a sure thing. Before it expired, I could sell my option to the developer and make a killing."

"What about your partner, the one that died."

"Ah, well…there wasn't really any partner."

"So you lied to me."

He nodded guiltily.

Samantha let that deception slide for the moment. "And you lost the money because you couldn't sell the option or buy the property yourself?"

"Yeah. All of it."

"Why didn't you tell me all this when you borrowed the money?" Samantha still couldn't see the connection between this and gambling.

"The payments for the option cost me more than I had, so I borrowed the rest from—from someone who charges a lot of interest."

"A loan shark?"

Boomer rose to his feet to start pacing, as if he could sit still no longer. "First I borrowed the ten thousand from you. I had an inside line on a couple of games that I thought I could make money on."

"You bet on Rainiers games? Ray, that's—"

"No." He stopped her. "I only bet on ones in the other division. But I lost that, too, so I borrowed ten thousand from Mom and Dad."

Samantha could see the pattern start to develop. "And you lost that, too." It was a statement.

"No, I won."

"What?"

"I won that time and another time after that, and I paid them back."

"Why didn't you stop, if you won?" Samantha cried.

"Because I needed more than ten thousand. I bet again and lost. So that's when I came to you for the other five thousand." He looked over at her, pleading. "I was on a roll, Sam. I thought I could win. And I did."

"You did?" Samantha was confused again.

He sighed and paced over to the window, staring out at the darkness. "It was a setup, Sam, a government sting. I figure they made sure I won and lost just enough to keep me coming back for more."

"They set up a sting to catch *you?*" Samantha asked incredulously.

Boomer snorted. "Hell, no. I was small potatoes compared to some of the guys hauled in there tonight. When this hits the news, there are going to be casualties scattered all over the city."

"Are any other players involved?"

"I don't think so. But some real high rollers got caught." Boomer rattled off some names.

Samantha recognized most of them. She was stunned. This might be as big a scandal as the Rainiers had ever experienced in their checkered history. Exactly the sort of thing that Elliott and she had worked to purge from the team's image. She propped her elbows on her knees and held her head in her hands.

"You've got to call Elliott, Ray. You have to tell him before he gets the story from the papers or television." Samantha raised her head and pinned her brother with a sharp stare. "I don't know if you're going to have a job after this."

Boomer didn't look surprised at her brutal words, just resigned. "Probably not."

Samantha brought the phone over to him and watched as he dialed the number. She put a hand on his shoulder and kept it there through the brief conversation, squeezing when she could see that it was a particularly hard moment. Boomer agreed to be at the club offices at eight o'clock the next morning and hung up.

"I guess that's it."

"What did he say?" Samantha asked quietly.

"He's going to have me come in for a meeting with the coaches and the lawyers." He paused and took a deep breath. "And I'm suspended, pending further investigation."

Samantha reached out and hugged him, her arms as tight

around him as they would go. Boomer finally broke down and
started to cry. It was an awful moment for them to share. All
she could do was rock him and hold him close. She had no
words to give him comfort.

JARRETT RANG SAMANTHA'S doorbell and waited, head down,
for her to open the door. *What a mess.* Before he left the courthouse, he had pulled Craig Miller aside to find out the details
of what Boomer had done. There was no pleasure in having
his poor opinion of Boomer James confirmed. He ached for
Samantha and how hurt she must be by her brother's stupidity.

The door swung open, pulling him away from his thoughts.
Seeing Samantha standing there, Jarrett felt a pang for the
romantic evening he had had planned and lost. How beautiful she was in her flowing green dress.

She offered him a tired, wan smile. "Hi, Jarrett. Come in."

She opened the door wide to let him pass. Jarrett stepped
forward and took her into his arms, holding her as he had in
the courthouse. She was tense, her body rigid against his. For
a moment she melted against him, but quickly drew away. As
she did, she wiped a tear from her cheek, trying to smile.

"Ray's gone to bed. At least that's what he said he was going
to do. I suspect he just didn't want to talk about it anymore."

"Did he call Elliott?"

"Yes. There's a meeting first thing in the morning."

Jarrett reached for Samantha again, but she turned and
walked into the living room and over to the window. Her back
to him, she said, "He's been suspended."

Jarrett sighed. He wished he could tell her that this was just
thunder from a passing storm, but he couldn't lie. Boomer had
really screwed up this time. There was a better than even
chance that this would end his baseball career, too. He went
to where she stood and slipped his hands around her waist,

pulling her back against his chest. Again, for just one moment, she softened and leaned on him. Seconds later she stiffened and pulled away, turning to face him.

"You shouldn't have come here tonight," Samantha said softly.

Jarrett frowned. "Why not?"

"Ray's in a lot of trouble," she began. "I have to stand by him. I can't let him go through this alone."

"Of course not, Sammy."

She looked away, then back, her eyes dark green and serious. "I have to stand by him, but I don't want you standing by him, too."

"Why not?" Jarrett said again, baffled.

"It's basic damage control. This is going to be a huge scandal, and Ray's going to be at the center of it. Anyone near him is bound to get some mud splattered on him. The fewer players associated with him, the cleaner the Rainiers will look after this. That includes you."

"Nobody's going to connect me with this scandal," he said. "I haven't got a thing to do with it."

"You heard those reporters tonight, Jarrett," Samantha argued. "They assumed you were arrested, too. Just because you were seen with me and Boomer."

"They're just sniffin' around for a story—"

"Exactly," she interrupted. "And your name will be in the paper right along with Boomer's and mine. You weren't a part of this mess, but you'll get smeared anyway." Samantha crossed her arms over her chest, hugging herself. "You have to stay away from me. We'll have our date when this dies down."

Anger rose in Jarrett. He couldn't believe what he was hearing. "If you think I'm abandoning you, you can forget it."

"It's not *abandoning* me." Her tone was cool. "It's just good business sense."

He grabbed her by the shoulders, pulling her to his chest. "To hell with the Rainiers," he said angrily. "I am *not* letting you go through this alone."

Jarrett glared down at her, furious that she could put the team first and their relationship second. After all he had been through to win her, how could she still set him aside for the sake of business?

"No, Jarrett." Samantha shook her head. Pushing away from him, she once again put the width of the room between them. "I don't want you to be a part of this."

"Samantha—"

She shook her head again. "Please leave."

He stared at her. She stood there so calm and intransigent. "I can't believe you're doing this. What does it take for you to stop thinking like a businesswoman and start thinking like a *woman* instead?" Jarrett laughed mirthlessly when she remained silent. "I'm through banging my head against this wall. You tell me I never take no for an answer? Fine. I'm taking it now."

He walked out of the condo, slamming the door behind him. She had pushed him away for the last time. The very last.

Chapter Fourteen

Samantha sat in the reception room of Andrew Elliott's office and tried not to fidget. She stared at a large, framed Rainiers logo on the wall across from her seat. Its bright red and blue design mesmerized her. She wondered how she could be so anxious, as exhausted as she was.

The image of Jarrett storming out had played repeatedly in her head all night. His angry words stabbed at her. *It was over.* She had known they were finished as soon as the door slammed behind him. Tears had come then, hot and fast. Finally, she had cried herself to sleep just before dawn.

When she had woken a couple of hours later, she pulled on a bathrobe and went out to find Boomer sitting on the balcony looking terribly alone. She had poured herself a cup of coffee and joined him.

"Good morning."

"'Morning," Boomer mumbled.

Samantha sat next to Boomer and put her hand over his. They linked fingers and sat, silent. After a while, he stirred.

"Will you drive me home so I can change before I meet with Elliott?" he asked.

"Sure," Samantha said, putting her coffee cup down. "I'll get dressed."

She took Boomer home, waited while he changed, then followed his car to the club offices. Craig and another attorney from his firm met them there to sit in on the meeting with Mr. Elliott and the senior coaches. Samantha had planned to leave then, but Mr. Elliott asked that she stay to meet with him afterward.

So here she sat, staring at the Rainier logo her company had designed, feeling stretched thin. It was hard to believe that just a few hours ago she had been anxious for a completely different reason. She closed her eyes and rotated her head, trying to ease some of the tension in her neck. The door to Elliott's office opened, and several men filed out, followed by Boomer and Craig. Samantha rose, looking from one to another, trying to read their faces.

She went to her brother and clasped his hand. "How did it go?" she asked quietly.

He shrugged. "About like I expected it. I'm suspended. They want to wait to see what the prosecutors do."

She turned to Craig, but, before she could speak, Andrew Elliott came out of the office. "Ms. James, I'd like to speak with you now."

Samantha squeezed Boomer's hand. "I'll talk to you later," she said. "Thanks, Craig."

Craig nodded and touched her arm. "Anytime."

Andrew Elliott held the door for Samantha, then closed it behind them.

"Please, have a seat."

When she had eased into one of his burgundy wingback chairs, he sat behind the desk, facing her. Samantha did not let her face reflect a twitch of the worry she felt. This was going to be difficult, but she hoped she could get through to the other side. Elliott was quiet for a moment. He steepled his fingers together, stared at her across the tops of them and frowned.

"What do you know about your brother's gambling?"

"Just what he told me last night. He got over his head in a real estate deal and resorted to gambling to pull himself out."

Elliott was again silent for a moment. "Boomer said you lent him money. Is that true?"

"Yes. He came to me on two separate occasions and asked to borrow money for the real estate deal."

"And you believed him?" Elliott was clearly skeptical.

"Yes, I believed him. He's my brother." Samantha felt her stomach do a slow, sick churn.

Elliott sat back in his chair. "I'm sorry for these questions, Samantha, but I wanted confirmation of what Boomer told us." Before she could speak, he continued, "As of this moment, I am canceling the Rainiers' contract with Emerald Advertising."

Samantha stared at him, stunned. The words echoed in her head as if coming from a great distance, but they didn't make sense. "What?"

Elliott stood and went to the window, then turned back to face her once more. "I warned you several times that I would deal with any scandal quickly and harshly. I will not have my team dragged through the mud again."

"Andrew, we can fix this."

Elliott cut her off. "No. Your involvement in this debacle makes you a liability. Your money funded Boomer's gambling, and the press will find that out sooner or later." He leveled a hard stare at Samantha. "You knew that any link to scandal would terminate our contract. It doesn't matter how deep your involvement or what your intentions. The club can no longer work with Emerald Advertising. I'm sorry, Samantha, but it's that simple."

Samantha's mind reeled from his words, trying to think of something to say, but she knew from Elliott's demeanor that this decision had been made. He would stick with it no matter what argument she made.

"Then there's nothing I can say to change your mind." It was her conclusion rather than a question. Elliott looked at her impassively, though Samantha thought she saw a glimmer of compassion in his faded eyes.

She stood, briefcase in hand, keeping her head up and her back straight. She would not let him see her broken.

"I'll have the final bill sent over to you on Monday morning." With those words, she left.

Samantha got into her car and drove automatically. She was in shock. Back at her office, she had no smile for Debbie as she handed over the morning's messages.

"Call everyone into the large conference room and put the phones on night-mode. I want you in on this meeting, too."

Debbie flashed her a worried look, but complied with the orders. Samantha went directly to the conference room, dropping her briefcase near the chair at the head of the table. She didn't sit. She just stared out the window with arms crossed, gathering her thoughts. Behind her, she heard everyone file in and quietly sit down. A tense silence hung over the room. The relaxed, creative atmosphere that had reigned the past few months had suddenly vanished.

Finally, Samantha turned and faced them. She looked at each person and felt infinitely sad. She had gambled on all their futures and lost.

"I'm sure you have all heard my brother was arrested last night for betting on baseball." There were nods and murmurs around the room. "I just met with Andrew Elliott. He has canceled the contract with us because of my connection to the scandal."

"What?" Lane exclaimed. "He can't do that. *You* weren't the one gambling."

Lane's defense warmed Samantha's heart. "I lent money to my brother that he used to place bets." She held up a hand to silence Lane before he could argue. "No. I *didn't* know he was going to use it for that. But, the fact remains that he used *my* money illegally. That was enough reason for Elliott to cut his losses and cancel our contract."

"So what does this all mean?" Pam asked.

Samantha sucked in a deep breath. She wished she could tell them anything other than what she was about to say. "It means that Emerald Advertising is in deep trouble. I don't know how bad it is, but it *will* be bad. We—I—pushed a lot of other work aside to take on this contract. It was almost more than we could handle, but you all did a fantastic job." She looked at each person. "Every one of you gave your best. You can be proud of that. But, in order to do this work, I didn't take on much else, so we have little to fall back on and not much in reserve. And, I don't know how much of our expenses the Rainiers will cover. I went ahead and ordered quite a bit of that work without authorization from them."

"If you'd waited for the bean counters to approve things, we'd be a month behind," Stuart interrupted with a snort.

"Yes, but those same bean counters may well decide that they don't have to pay for work that was done without their say-so." She sighed. "I have to run the numbers, but I'm pretty sure we'll be well into the red."

"Then we just have to hang on until we get more work," Lane said stubbornly.

"*If* we get more work," Samantha qualified. "I'm going to be at the center of this scandal, guys. My brother is involved and I can't—won't—let him stand alone while he goes through it. Even if I did abandon him, I would still be part of the talk. We're in the image business," she added, looking around the room at the serious faces before her. "Who wants to buy an image from a company whose own image is tarnished?"

No one had an answer for that. Finally, Samantha sat folding her hands on the table in front of her. "So, it's going to be bad. I'll know exactly how bad on Monday. I suggest that you all take the rest of today and the weekend to think about your options. I won't be offended if you use the time to work on your résumés."

"But, Samantha—"

"Not today, Lane. Go home and try to relax. Take this as the break that you most definitely need and deserve. If you come up with any brilliant ideas to save our hides, I'll be here Monday at eight."

Samantha stayed seated as, after a pause, her staff rose and left the room as quietly as they had entered. She sat back and rubbed a hand over her forehead. She wanted to think the worst was over, but she knew it wasn't going to be that easy. She still had to crunch some numbers to learn how bad the catastrophe was going to be.

She sat for a time, gazing blankly at the far wall, but finally stood and went to her office, taking her briefcase and the messages Debbie had given her earlier. The back office was quiet—everyone had taken her advice and gone home. Sitting at her desk, she leafed through the message slips, many of them from reporters, others from clients and friends.

She set the rest of the messages aside and faced the inevitable, calling up the Rainiers file on her computer. The numbers there told her what she already knew: Emerald Advertising was finished. Too much money out and not enough coming in to cover the gap. Her fatal mistake was assuming that the contract would last the season. Ignoring the cancellation clause, she had moved ahead on three new commercial spots. In her confidence, she had her people, as well as the director's crew, working on the production. She had the printer laying up a new program.

All that work already done, all that money already owed. There was no way the Rainiers would cover it all, since they wouldn't see the final product. Emerald Advertising, not the Rainiers, would have to pay for it. Then there was the matter of the loan from the bank. How would she repay that? Her reserves were minimal. The money she had lent Ray had vanished permanently, that was certain. Without income from the Rainiers, any extra funds she had would quickly be eaten up by payroll and rent.

Samantha sat back and stared at the computer screen. She laughed mirthlessly. The sound echoed through the quiet office and sent a shiver along her skin. She had gambled and lost. She had gotten so arrogant and cocky that she ignored the risks. She was just like Boomer. They had both bet and lost everything.

With nothing else to do, she turned off the computer and collected her briefcase. As she walked through the empty offices, she took a long, last look at her tiny empire. It broke her heart to think that it would die. But what choice was there? She turned off the lights, locked the door behind her and left the building. She had two days to plan for the future, but that future looked bleak and empty right now.

She drove home slowly. Once there, she wandered from room to room, looking for something to occupy her hands and her head. She brewed herself a cup of chamomile tea and sipped it while hashing through the morning's events and worrying about the future.

Slowly, anger began to come in and replace the gloom. Why was she being punished for a crime she had no real part in committing? Andrew Elliott was wrong. Samantha had done nothing dishonest. If she was to be faulted for anything it was for believing in her no-account brother.

How dare Elliott blame her for this fiasco? Samantha took her cup of tea to the kitchen and dumped it in the sink. She could do nothing about the end of Emerald Advertising, but she refused to let Andrew Elliott make her ashamed. She would hold her head up high, despite anything he or the press might say about her involvement in the scandal.

That decided, Samantha strode to her bedroom and changed into slacks and a sleeveless sweater. She freshened her makeup, brushed her hair and pulled it back in a loose ponytail. Staring at herself in the mirror, she saw the glint of anger and determination in her own eyes and nodded at herself. It was better to be fierce and go down fighting. Much better.

She picked up the phone and dialed the clubhouse. "May I speak to Peter Brinks?"

JARRETT WALKED INTO THE locker room, grabbed a towel off a stack near the door and wiped his sweaty face. He went to his locker and sat on the bench in front of it with a sigh, rubbing his aching shoulder. He was bone-tired.

After a near-sleepless night, Jarrett had come to the ballpark to work off some of the anger and hurt he felt toward Samantha. Her rejection burned like a brand. He had hoped sheer physical exertion would wipe his mind of her, but it hadn't. With all his thoughts consumed by her, his pitching had been terrible. She truly was his lucky charm, and she had taken all the luck and charm with her.

He flipped off his hat and bent to unlace his shoes. Around him, other players changed into or out of uniforms. The usual cacophony of the team was subdued to a murmur. Here and there, clumps of men gathered for hushed conversations. Rumors were running rampant. The grapevine had already yielded the news of Boomer's suspension that morning.

Jarrett stripped off his sweaty practice uniform and headed for the whirlpool. Halfway there, he ran into Peter Brinks.

"Hey, Peter."

"Hey, Jarrett. How's it going?"

"Could be worse," Jarrett said with a slight smile. "Any news from upstairs?"

Peter shook his head. "Nothing from them, but I did talk to your girlfriend, Samantha James, a few minutes ago. You must be pissed."

Jarrett frowned. He couldn't believe Samantha would tell the clubhouse man about their fight. "She told you?"

"Well, yeah," Peter said, then he lowered his voice. "You want my opinion? Elliott's gone off his rocker with this one. I mean, firing her is going too far."

"What? He *fired* Samantha?"

Peter's eyes widened. "You didn't know?"

Jarrett grabbed the man by the arm and pulled him into the relative privacy of the whirlpool room. "What did she say?" he demanded. "Tell me everything."

As he listened to Peter, Jarrett's alarm grew. Everything Samantha had ever said about Andrew Elliott's threats came back to him in a rush. She had been right all along. Elliott's threats weren't empty. He had actually fired her for innocently helping her brother with a loan.

Suddenly, her reasons for pushing him away were cast in a new light. Samantha wasn't rejecting him, she was *protecting* him. She knew Elliott would go off the deep end and she wanted to shield him from what she knew would come. It wasn't business: it was love.

At least, he hoped so.

Jarrett remembered his own hurled accusations and felt sick. The one time he had taken "no" for an answer left her standing alone to face this storm. The thought made his heart ache. At the same time, it filled him with new determination. He had worked hard to win her. There was no way he was giving up now. Peter's voice interrupted Jarrett's reverie.

"So, I told her I hadn't heard anything about her tickets being canceled and she should come to the game tonight."

"She's coming to the game?"

"That's what she said."

"Thanks, Peter," Jarrett said, squeezing the other man's shoulder. "Do me another favor and keep all this to yourself for a while."

"Sure, Jarrett," Peter agreed. "I wouldn't have said anything, but I thought you already knew."

"I've been practicing all morning. Samantha's probably been trying to get a hold of me," Jarrett lied smoothly.

Peter nodded and the two men parted. Jarrett walked to the whirlpool and slipped into the hot water. As the jets pummeled his muscles, his mind reeled at the news Peter had told him.

Damn Andrew Elliott.

He was nuts to believe anyone would blame Samantha for Boomer's stupid stunt just because she lent her brother money. And couldn't Elliott see that the team needed good advertising now more than ever?

Jarrett closed his eyes. All the good publicity their "dating game" had sparked would go to waste. He smiled, thinking how his gambles to win Samantha had paid off in the newspapers. He had played his cards right. Boomer was not so lucky. Or not so skilled. His eyes opened again. Maybe that was the answer. There *was* a way to get Elliott to change his mind. It was risky, but it could work. The right cards, played just the right way…

Jarrett pulled himself out of the whirlpool and toweled off. He had to act quickly. He had one last gamble to make to win the woman he loved. And he *would* win. For both of them.

Chapter Fifteen

Just before game time, Samantha got out of her car at Sicks
Stadium. She had made the decision to come to the game, but
actually going *inside* the stadium was daunting. She had stalled
as long as she could and now, with the first pitch moments
away, she knew she could do so no longer. Thoughts about
swarms of curious—even scornful—spectators who awaited
her made her faintly ill. Still, she knew she had to do this.

At the entrance, a woman scanned her season ticket, the
one of two that Elliott had personally handed to her at the beginning of the year. Samantha tensed as she waited for it to
be rejected. It wasn't, and she walked slowly up into the
stands, just as the national anthem played. The stares and
gawks that had accompanied her the last time returned in full
force. This time they seemed to hold a coolness, even an
enmity. She was uncomfortable, but refused to show it. This
was far harder than she had thought.

She found her seat and sat, trying to ignore the world. It
was nearly impossible, but she managed to keep her composure. She flipped through her program and kept her eyes on
the field, speaking to no one, meeting no one's eyes. Keeping
up the pretense was work. The progress of the game barely
registered in her head. She couldn't keep herself from looking

fór Jarrett, though he wasn't pitching tonight. Soon it was the bottom of the sixth inning.

What finally caught Samantha's attention was a rustling in the seats around her. She kept her eyes on the infield, but could see nothing out of the ordinary. The players were in position and the game played out as usual. Then she noticed movement to her left and saw Ben Rosenthal and Brad Swift, both relief pitchers, enter the stands from the field. One of them pointed to her. Seeing that they had gotten her attention, they beckoned her over to them. Samantha felt like hiding under her seat, but they waved more insistently and headed her way, so she stood.

"What's the problem, guys?"

"Nothing, Samantha. Jarrett just wants to see you for a minute."

Samantha grew alarmed. After their last stormy encounter, she couldn't imagine what Jarrett would want with her now. It hardly seemed like the time or place to resume their argument.

"What? Why does he want to see me? Why didn't he come himself?"

The players both shrugged and grinned. "Don't know," Rosenthal said. "He just asked us to come get you."

"Come on, Samantha," Swift cajoled. "Just for a minute. Be a pal."

She frowned, but reluctantly let them usher her out of the stands. The camera in the second tier followed them. At least she would get away from its glassy-eyed intrusion. Her escorts led her past the concession stands and down into the depths of the stadium. They turned into a section of the building she had been in only once and, that time, briefly. Ahead lay a narrow passageway that led to the dugout. Here, she balked.

"What's going on? Where are you taking me?" she demanded.

The two men smiled. "Don't worry. We're just taking you to Jarrett."

She looked at them suspiciously, but could think of no reason to doubt them. Yet, when her eyes readjusted to the bright glare of the stadium lights, she saw that the dugout was empty. She might have dashed back into the tunnel, but the pitchers each grasped one of her elbows and led her up the steps onto the playing field. She blinked in utter astonishment.

There before her were the Rainiers strung out in two parallel lines that ended at the pitcher's mound. They faced in toward each other, like some processional honor guard. The aisle formed between them was just wide enough for Samantha and her escorts to walk through. Each man, coaches included, wore a wide grin and held his hat over his heart.

Overhead, the announcer's voice blared out of the stadium speakers, "And now, ladies and gentlemen, we have a surprise tonight and a special guest, as the Rainiers welcome Samantha James to the field. As you all know, our starting pitcher, Jarrett Corliss, won a date with the lovely lady and that sent the Rainiers to the top of the standings. Give her a big round of applause for being such a good influence on our team."

The crowd roared its approval. Startled to hear her name, Samantha stopped dead, but Rosenthal and Swift urged her along.

"So tonight," the announcer continued, "Jarrett and the team want to honor her with a special gift."

At the end of the row, Samantha saw Jarrett on the mound. He was up to some grand trick, and she was walking straight into it. But it was too late to turn and flee. Whatever it was, he had certainly outdone himself. She let herself be walked down the gauntlet of smirking baseball players.

At the crest of dirt, her escorts left her side to stand in line with the other players. Jarrett grinned at her and held out his hand. She gingerly put hers into it and was pulled to the top of the mound by his side. Then he pulled off his own hat, placed it over his heart and dropped to one knee in front of her. Their image flashed on all the screens around the stadium. Again, the crowd went wild. Jarrett gazed up at her, mischief in his dimpled smile. Samantha opened her mouth to speak, but realized nothing could be heard over the cheering of the fans. Finally, the noise level dropped.

"Jarrett, get up," she implored anxiously.

Jarrett cleared his throat, ignoring her request. "Samantha, I love you. I have since the first day we met and I will until the day I die."

"Jarrett Corliss, are you completely nuts? This is not the place for this. What are you doing?"

"Samantha, would you do me the honor of becoming my wife?"

"What?" This question caught her completely off guard, sending her head into an even greater spin than it already was.

Jarrett fished into his pants pocket. He withdrew a small, velvet-covered box and offered it to her. "This is for you."

Samantha looked at the box and then at Jarrett. She took it, lifted the lid and gasped. Nestled in the plush interior was a gold ring with a perfect two-karat emerald surrounded by small diamonds.

"Jarrett, it's beautiful."

Jarrett, still kneeling, took the ring and slid it on the third finger of her left hand. He then kissed the spot and clasped her hand in his again.

"Samantha James, please marry me."

The stadium erupted in cheers and applause once more. Samantha looked up. Above her, she could see the lighted message board flash Samantha James, Please Marry Me in five-foot-tall letters. She looked back down at him kneeling in the dust before her and said the words in her heart.

"I love you, Jarrett." She laughed in helpless delight. "You're crazy, but I love you."

He couldn't hear her speak, the noise from the fans was too loud, but he saw the words form on her lips. He stood and swept her into his arms. Wild applause and raucous cheers greeted his actions. The noise was more deafening, and Samantha stood on tiptoe to shout in Jarrett's ear.

"Yes! I will marry you!"

Jarrett pulled back far enough to capture her lips with his in a kiss.

"Folks, I think that's a yes," the announcer spoke over the din.

"Goin' to the Chapel" blared from the organ as the crowds went even wilder. The team broke formation and joined in the celebration with yells and hats tossed high into the sky. Then, before complete chaos burst out, the players escorted Jarrett and Samantha off the field. Once in the dugout, Jarrett accepted the congratulations of his comrades. Then he whisked Samantha out of the stadium. In his car, driving away, she finally regained her senses.

"Wait a minute, Jarrett. My car's still back there."

"We'll pick it up tomorrow." He kept driving.

Samantha sat back and regarded her new fiancé. "Did I really just agree to marry you in front of all those screaming people at a baseball game?"

"Yep."

"Are you sure?"

"You're not getting out of it, Sam. I've got thirty *thousand* witnesses to prove that you said yes."

"Who said anything about backing out?" She looked over at him with tears of happiness in her eyes. "Pull over."

Jarrett obeyed and guided the car to the side of the road and shifted into neutral. Samantha slid her arms around his neck and gave him a long, luxurious kiss. Jarrett pulled her against him as if he would never let go. Though the gearshift dug into her thigh, she knew it was the sweetest kiss they had ever shared.

"I love you, Jarrett. You've made me the happiest woman in the world."

He kissed her again, quick and hard. "I love you, too, darlin'. I hope you won't ever stop."

"Never," she breathed, and they did not speak for a long while.

Finally Jarrett lifted his head and set her back in her own seat. He shifted into first gear and set them in motion once more. Samantha turned sideways in her seat to look at him as he drove. He put his hand over hers, stroking a thumb over the ring before linking their fingers together. Samantha gazed down at their joined hands and smiled. It was a wonder to her that she could go from the depths of despair to the heights of happiness in twenty-four hours. The future suddenly looked bright.

In her condo, Samantha pulled Jarrett out of his uniform, throwing clothes in every direction to get down to bare skin. Their lovemaking was fierce. They were staking a claim and declaring their rights to each other. The sky was overcast, but together they pushed the clouds apart and touched the stars.

Eventually, the rush of pleasure faded, and Samantha found herself earthbound once more. Her worries about her business returned, looming over her and Jarrett's happiness, but she refused to let them dim this moment of delight. Jarrett's muscular arm lay over her chest, and one hand gently cupped her breast. She felt his tenderness and strength all at once. She may have lost her company, but she had gained something priceless. She glanced at the ring on her finger, the token of his love for her. It sparkled and glowed, a beacon of hope. A future without her company was sad, but bearable. She had something better.

"Oh, I forgot to tell you something. There's more that goes with that ring."

She shifted to look at Jarrett. "More? What more could there be? I have all I want or deserve right here."

Jarrett smiled and pressed a kiss to her lips. His pleasure at her answer was apparent. "*I* think you deserve more. That's why I proposed to you at the game in front of all those fans."

"What do you mean?"

"I had a little chat with Andrew Elliott."

Samantha was confused. "What does he have to do with my ring?"

"Peter told me earlier that you'd been fired. You should have called me, Sammy."

"I wanted to, but—" She looked away. "I didn't want you tarred with the same brush as Ray."

Jarrett pulled her into his arms and held her tightly. "I'm sorry about last night," he began. "I was hurt and I lashed back at you. I—"

Samantha stopped his words with a warm kiss. "We both made a mistake last night. Let's forget about it."

Jarrett cupped her face in his hands and kissed her deeply. Samantha's heart sang with happiness. He lifted his lips from hers and rose on one elbow.

"So I talked with Elliott," he repeated.

"What about?"

"Well, first off, I told him he was wrong to cancel your contract."

"What?" She couldn't believe her ears. No one had ever loved her this much. She hugged him fiercely, touched by his protectiveness. "Thank you, Jarrett. That was very sweet of you."

"Yeah, well, you may not think it's too sweet when you hear the rest."

Samantha sat up. "What *rest?*"

Jarrett grinned, sitting up to face her. "I'm almost afraid to tell you. You might accuse me of blackmail again."

"What did you do now?"

"I convinced Elliott to keep Emerald Advertising on the job for the rest of the season."

Samantha looked at him in amazement, and the feeling quickly changed to delight. "You did?" She threw her arms around him in an ecstatic embrace, then pulled back to look at him in wonder. "Jarrett! How did you—"

He cut her off with a kiss. "Hold on, darlin'. It's not all that simple." When she had calmed down, he said, "I told Elliott that he was wrong to fire you for supporting your brother. You didn't know what he was up to anyway."

"But he doesn't care about that."

"He *didn't* care about that," Jarrett corrected. "Until I showed him why he should."

"What do you mean?"

"Well, I played a little game of make-believe poker with ol' Andy. I reminded him how well I've been pitching lately and told him how much that has to do with you. I told him to call the pitching coach and ask about that time you came to the stadium. You didn't believe me when I told you my pitching got better when I saw you, but it's the truth. You always make my game better."

Samantha kissed him. "Thank you, Jarrett, but—"

"Now, hold on, Sammy," he interrupted. "I'm not finished layin' my cards out here. Elliott wasn't too happy to hear how sore my arm was and how I didn't know if I could go on pitching well, since you were so unhappy." He grinned, obviously remembering the scene. "I also told him that I didn't know if we could keep from telling the press our side of the story. They want to know everything about us these days."

Samantha frowned. "Our side of *what* story?"

Jarrett's eyes were a wide, innocent blue, a look she knew too well. "Why, how you were fired for standing by your brother in his time of need," he said solemnly. "How you trusted your brother and he let you down, but *you* couldn't do the same to him, no matter what he'd done. And, for that, you lost your contract with the team and would probably have to *lay people off* or even *close your doors*." As he ended this dramatic speech, the dimple in his cheek winked.

"You didn't!" she said.

"Well, I've got a lot of friends in the press, Sammy. I think we'd get one or two of those reporters to listen to us. Elliott wouldn't come out lookin' too good, which I was honor-bound to point out to him. Just imagine the storyline," he mused, eyes closed. "Heartless team owner axes the brave young businesswoman because she helped her poor brother." His eyes opened and a glint of pure devilishness shone in the blue depths. "It's got a nice ring to it."

Samantha's mouth dropped open in astonishment. She remembered all too clearly the stories Jarrett wove for the press during their challenge. "And he fell for it?"

"Well, he wasn't a pushover. He argued that I couldn't guarantee my arm would hold up, even if you were happy. And that the press would still talk about your relationship to Boomer and the money thing would come out. He had some good points, so I had to make some concessions," Jarrett added.

"Concessions?"

"He is the boss, you know," Jarrett quipped. "I made a deal with him. If I continue to pitch well and the team makes it to the playoffs, you get paid for everything. If we don't, you only get reimbursed for your costs. I had to think on my feet, Sam," he said, looking deeply into her eyes. "I hope I didn't promise too much."

Samantha ran a hand through her hair, her mind in a whirl.

Win or lose, the concession was worlds better than her present situation. "No, Jarrett. Anything is better than nothing."

"I also had an idea that would take everyone's mind off Boomer. When I mentioned that, ol' Elliott's big ears perked right up." Jarrett chuckled. "I said I'd provide one more free round of advertising for him."

"So you told him that you were going to propose to me at the game?"

"Well, I didn't tell him *what* I was going to do, just that I would do something dramatic that the fans would love. I did tell him we were about to be engaged and let his imagination do the rest. I didn't want to spoil the surprise." Jarrett snickered at his own prank.

Samantha hugged him. "Jarrett, you lying rascal, you did all this for me?"

"For us," he said against her throat.

He slid down to lie prone in the rumpled sheets, pulling her with him. He placed a trail of kisses over her shoulder, nibbling a pathway of fire. Samantha was moved to happiness and joy beyond words. He had given her back her dream. Over the lump in her throat, she whispered to him, "You were right all along, Jarrett Corliss. Nobody can have just one dream."

Jarrett raised his head from the necklace of kisses he was stringing around her throat and shoulders. "What other dreams do you have, Sammy?"

"You." Samantha stroked a hand through his blond hair, feeling the silken strands against her palm. "You're my dream."

He kissed her lips tenderly and soon the only sounds in the room were soft moans and whispers of love. A while later, Samantha was in high spirits, studying her ring and teasing Jarrett once again.

"So you only proposed to me to pressure Elliott to keep Emerald on with the team. Is that right?"

"No, Sammy, I had planned to do that after I won the last game of your challenge. I worked so hard to win, I decided I'd keep you." He laughed when she pinched him. "Then, when I was thinking about how to convince Elliott, it all came together."

"I suppose we've done everything else in public. Why not our engagement, too?"

"There you go. That's what I thought. It seemed like the perfect decoy for Boomer and his gambling. I was going to propose to you someday. I just moved it up."

Samantha smiled mistily at this man that loved her so thoroughly. "I do love you, Jarrett. More than I could ever say."

Jarrett responded with a fiery kiss. Poised over her, he sobered again. "But it still means your company is out on a limb. I can't guarantee that we'll win. I talked to the team about the whole deal and they're behind us, one hundred percent."

"You told the team—" Samantha stopped. "Well, I don't care how far out we are, I can pull us back in, now that I have a chance. You'll make it, Jarrett, and you'll win," she declared, smacking a kiss on his mouth. "Because we're not going to get married until you do."

"What?" he asked, and blinked at her in confusion.

"A pennant would make such a lovely wedding present, don't you think?"

"Sam—" Jarrett protested, but she cut him off.

"Jarrett, I know you can do it, *darlin'*," she teased, using her best imitation of his drawl.

"You didn't mean that, did you? I mean about not getting married if we don't *win* the playoffs?"

Samantha smiled up at his stunned look. "You worry too much, you know that?"

"You *do* mean it," he said, incredulous. "Sam, I can't possibly—"

Samantha pulled his head down to hers and showed him just how possible some things were.

Much, much later he lay sated, panting slightly. "Don't you ever accuse me of blackmail again. I've got miles to go before I catch up with you."

Samantha laughed as she rested her head against his warm, damp stomach. She couldn't wait to tell the world about their wedding plans. This news would make the best headline yet.

Chapter Sixteen

Samantha sat in the stands watching Jarrett warm up. He would pitch in this final game of the playoffs. So far the games had been close. First the Rainiers took the lead, then Oakland, then the Rainiers tied the series. This game would decide which team was the most worthy. Samantha was nearly vibrating with tension.

Brenda laughed. "Calm down, Samantha. He'll do fine. You're not going to pass out on me, are you? Craig, give me one of those paper bags."

Samantha shot Brenda a look of panic, ignoring the teasing. "I should have never told him I wouldn't marry him unless he won the playoffs, Bren. What was I thinking?"

Brenda only laughed again at her friend's anxiety and offered her a bag of peanuts. Samantha took the bag, grateful to have something to do with her hands as she automatically cracked open the shells and dropped the nuts into Brenda's outstretched palm. Eating was beyond her right now.

Since returning to the office, Brenda complained daily about the mountain of paperwork Samantha had saved for her. Samantha had hugged her tightly the day she returned and promised a raise if she never left again. Brenda grumbled, but was obviously pleased that she was so badly needed. The baby was in a day care close by, and Samantha encouraged her to spend as much time with Katie as possible. Anything to keep Brenda content at work. Samantha didn't want to run the show without her ever again.

The past months had been a mixture of work and play. Jarrett was on the road as much as he was home. Each moment they spent together was precious. As the team progressed game by game to the playoffs, Jarrett had spent more time at practice and in sessions analyzing tapes of previous games. He had sat out several games in the middle of July because of stress to his shoulder. He behaved like a bear with a sore paw all through it. Samantha had actually been glad to send him back out on the road, recovered and pitching well.

He and Samantha had learned to balance their lives together. If Jarrett and the team played in Seattle, Samantha attended the game. The few nights he didn't have to be at the club they spent together, often alone at home laughing, talking and loving. She tried to make the weekend away games, but they made for long, exhausting trips. She didn't know how the team could keep going from city to city. One weekend on the road wore her out. When she stayed behind in Seattle, or traveled on her own business, they would spend hours on the phone, trying to share an intimate moment a thousand miles apart. At least the team was doing well. That was Samantha's small consolation when she would rather have Jarrett home with her.

Just as the Rainiers progressed, Emerald Advertising did, too. With the payments from the club assured and three lucrative new contracts secured, the company was back on stable footing. Her dealings with Andrew Elliott had been tense at first. He was not happy at all about Jarrett's "extortion," as he called it. It took a while, but he finally admitted that keeping Emerald Advertising was a wise move. And Jarrett's proposal on the pitcher's mound had engendered tremendous support for the team. The anticipated slump in ticket sales after the gambling scandal never occurred.

As the season came to a close, Samantha was working on a campaign for the next year. She had signed a two-year contract with the Rainiers for more money than she had ever hoped of getting out of the once-stumbling team. Elliott had announced that he had no plans to move the club to another city. They had had a tremendously successful year, and he planned to roll the financial gains back into the ball club to ensure its long-term success.

Among other things, that meant Jarrett received a new contract with the team—three years at a salary that would insure his financial security. He and Samantha were living in her condo while they looked for a house to buy.

All those hurdles led to this one game. Tonight was the moment they had worked for all summer. Tonight history would be made. Or not. Samantha had never expected to worry about a baseball game this much. Of course, she had never had so much riding on one, either. After she and Jarrett got engaged and Samantha announced that she would marry Jarrett if he won the pennant, the pressure had begun to mount. It climbed with every win and doubled with every loss.

"Hey, Samantha," a voice above her in the stands cried. "Have you ordered the wedding cake yet?"

Samantha turned and looked up at the young man hanging over the rail around the VIP section. She smiled and crossed her fingers, then turned back around. It wasn't the first time she'd been asked that sort of question today. She had answered all of them positively, hiding her true concerns.

The wedding challenge had made the front page of all the local papers and graced the sports sections in most of the national papers as well. The public loved it. Even Andrew Elliott had gotten into the spirit. The couple was the best moneymaker he'd had in years, bringing in truckloads of cash at no cost. Eventually, he claimed that the idea had been his all along. Samantha smiled to herself and let the man bluster. She knew the truth.

It was ridiculous and wonderful at the same time. Samantha had known that being Jarrett's wife was going to mean time in the spotlight, but she hadn't planned it quite this way. They had conducted one of the most public courtships in Seattle history. Still, the jokes were told in fun, and the team *was* having an incredible winning season.

The only dim spot on this bright September day was Boomer's absence from the field. He had been found guilty, along with other public figures, of illegal betting on baseball games. Since it was his first offense, he was sentenced to community service. He had taken the fall from grace hard and was working diligently to turn his life around. And though he was suspended from play, there was a chance he would be eligible for next season. Samantha found that she liked him more now. Jarrett also had gone out of his way to make her brother feel welcome in their home. Samantha couldn't say whether he would ever like Boomer entirely, but the two men seemed to have reached an understanding.

"Peanuts! Get yer peanuts!" came the yells of the vendors. They tossed foil bags of warm peanuts to customers across ten rows of seats. Samantha had teased Jarrett, after a game that he had not pitched well, that he ought to take lessons from the peanut vendors—they were better at hitting their target than he was. Jarrett had laughed, drawn out of his blue mood.

The national anthem played, the players took the field and the mayor threw out the first ball. Samantha waved to Jarrett when his head swiveled up to the stands where she was seated. Before he started any game, he had gotten in the habit of picking her out in the stands. She felt the same rush of love and pride that she felt whenever he looked for her here.

The first hitter for Oakland came to the plate, and Samantha focused her attention on the game. She saw in the first few windups that Jarrett was pitching well. Hopefully, he could keep the pace going. She had wished, in the past few games, that by focusing on Jarrett she could somehow transmit some of her strength to him as he gave his all on the field.

The first inning finished quickly. Jarrett had not let a run in. Yet when the Rainiers stepped up to the plate, they, too, were kept scoreless. The second and third innings went the same way. Jarrett was pitching well, the team pulling hard together, but Oakland was matching them.

The fourth inning broke the standoff. Scott Seibert, the Rainiers' designated hitter, pounded one into the left-field stands. The home run drove the crowd into a frenzy. The sound of stomping, cheering and clapping was deafening. The fifth and sixth innings were a repeat of the earlier ones with no score for either team. Samantha wondered if Ben Rosenthal would relieve Jarrett. It would depend on Jarrett's shoulder and how it was holding up under the pressure. So far he had pitched a perfect game. No one could fault that.

All too quickly the seventh stretch came up. Samantha stood with the rest of the crowd. She eased the tension she felt in her neck, twisting and turning it until the kinks unlocked. Jarrett was hanging in there. The score was 1-0 in favor of the Rainiers and, so far, not one of the Oakland players had made it safely to first base. It looked like Jarrett might pitch the best game of his life.

Bottom of the seventh, and the Rainiers failed to score. Top of the eighth, the Rainiers kept Oakland from getting a run. The inning was over. Bottom of the eighth, the Rainiers brought another run in, gaining a two-run lead. The crowd

roared in approval. Top of the ninth, Oakland's last chance at
bat. If they didn't score, the Rainiers won the pennant. Jarrett
wound up for the pitch. It sizzled by the batter. Strike one. Two
more followed and the batter was out. Samantha gripped her
fingers tightly together.

The next batter stepped up to the plate and cocked his bat.
Jarrett surveyed his opponent, watched the catcher's signal,
nodded at his choice and fired the ball. Strike again. Samantha
was at the edge of her seat, along with the entire stadium. They
were inches from victory. Two more whizzed from the mound
across the plate, both balls. There were several moans and a
tense hush. Had Jarrett worn himself out? The fourth and
fifth pitches followed, proving that he had not. They were both
strikes and another batter walked away from the plate, cursing.

The third, and hopefully the final, batter stepped into the box
and dug in his cleats. Batter and pitcher eyed one another over
the distance. Jarrett flung first one and then two strikes. Over
thirty thousand fans were going crazy from the hope and tension.
Samantha was on her feet, too, shouting her encouragement.
Jarrett seemed to hear her above everyone else, because he
stepped back and gazed up at the section of seats where she was
standing. He tipped his hat and threw the next pitch.

As soon as the ball left Jarrett's hand the crowd quieted a
fraction. They seemed to hold their collective breath as the
ball traveled out of his hand, over the grass toward home
plate. Samantha thought it was the fastest ball he had ever
thrown. It was over the plate, and the batter swung. Samantha
heard the satisfying sound as the ball slapped the catcher's
mitt. Strike three!

Jarrett had pitched a perfect game.

The Rainiers had won the pennant.

Pandemonium broke out. Above the jubilant sounds, the
stadium organist played, not the Rainiers' usual victory song,

but the wedding march. Tears of joy cascaded down Samantha's cheeks. For her, Jarrett had won much more than a league pennant. He had won their future and all her love.

* * * * *

Love Inspired
HISTORICAL

*Powerful, engaging stories of romance, adventure and faith
set in the past—when life was simpler and faith played a
major role in everyday lives.*

*See below for a sneak preview of
HIGH COUNTRY BRIDE
by Jillian Hart*

*Love Inspired Historical—love and faith
throughout the ages*

Silence remained between them, and she felt the rake of his gaze, taking her in from the top of her wind-blown hair where escaped tendrils snapped in the wind to the toe of her scuffed, patched shoes. She watched him fist up his big, work-roughened hands and expected the worst.

"You never told me, Miz Nelson. Where are you going to go?" His tone was flat, his jaw tensed as if he were still fighting his temper. His blue gaze shot past her to watch the children going about their picking up.

"I don't know." Her throat went dry. Her tongue felt thick as she answered. "When I find employment, I could wire a payment to you. Rent. Y-you aren't think-ing of bringing the sher-iff in?"

"You think I want *payment?*" He boomed like winter thunder. *"You think I want rent money?"*

"Frankly, I don't know what you want."

"I'll tell you what I don't want. I don't want—" His words cannoned in the silence as he paused, and a passing pair of geese overhead honked in flat-noted tones. He grimaced, and it was impossible to know what he would say or do.

She trembled, not from fear of him, she truly didn't believe he would strike her, but from the unknown. Of being forced to take the frightening step off the only safe spot she'd known since she'd lost Pa's house.

When you were homeless, everything seemed so fragile, so easily off balance, for it was a big, unkind world for a woman alone with her children. She had no one to protect her. No one to care. The truth was, she'd never had those things in her husband. How could she expect them from any stranger? Especially this man she hardly knew, who was harsh and cold and hard-hearted.

And, worse, what if he brought in the law?

"You can't keep living out of a wagon," he said, still angry, the cords still straining in his neck. "Animals have enough sense to keep their young cared for and safe."

Yes, it was as she'd thought. He intended to be as cruel about this as he could be. She spun on her heel, pulling up all her defenses, and was determined to let his upcoming hurtful words roll off her like rainwater on an oiled tarp. She grabbed the towel the children had neatly folded and tossed it into the laundry box in the back of the wagon.

"Miz Nelson. I'm talking to you."

"Yes, I know. If you expect me to stand there while you tongue-lash me, you're mistaken. I have packing to get to." Her fingers were clumsy as she hefted the bucket of water she'd brought for washing—she wouldn't need that now—and heaved.

His hand clasped on the handle beside hers, and she could feel the life and power of him vibrate along the thin metal. "Give it to me."

Her fingers let go. She felt stunned as he walked away, easily carrying the bucket that had been so heavy to her, and quietly, methodically, put out the small cooking fire. He did not seem as ominous or as intimidating—somehow—as he stood in the shadows, bent to his task, although she couldn't say why that was. Perhaps it was because he wasn't acting the way she was used to men acting. She was quite used to doing all the work.

Jamie scurried over, juggling his wooden horses, to watch. Daisy hung back, eyes wide and still, taking in the mysterious goings-on.

He is different when he's near to them, she realized. He didn't seem harsh, and there was no hint of anger—or, come to think of it, any other emotion—as he shook out the empty bucket, nodded once to the children and then retraced his path to her.

"Let me guess." He dropped the bucket onto the tailgate, and his anger appeared to be back. Cords strained in his neck and jaw as he growled at her. "If you leave here, you don't know where you're going and you have no money to get there with?"

She nodded. "Yes, sir."

"Then get you and your kids into the wagon. I'll hitch up your horses for you." His eyes were cold and yet they were not unfeeling as he fastened his gaze on hers. "I have an empty shanty out back of my house that no one's living in. You can stay there for the night."

"What?" She stumbled back, and the solid wood of the tailgate bit into the small of her back. "But—"

"There will be no argument," he bit out, interrupting her. "None at all. I buried a wife and son years ago, what was most precious to me, and to see you and them neglected like this—with no one to care—" His jaw ground again and his eyes were no longer cold.

Joanna didn't think she'd ever seen anything sadder than Aiden McKaslin as the sun went down on him.

* * * * *

Don't miss this deeply moving story,
HIGH COUNTRY BRIDE,
available July 2008
from the new Love Inspired Historical line.

Also look for SEASIDE CINDERELLA
by Anna Schmidt,
where a poor servant girl and a wealthy merchant prince
might somehow make a life together.

REQUEST YOUR FREE BOOKS!

2 FREE NOVELS PLUS 2
FREE GIFTS!

Heart, Home & Happiness!

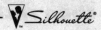

SPECIAL EDITION™

NEW YORK TIMES
BESTSELLING AUTHOR

DIANA
PALMER

A brand-new Long, Tall Texans novel

HEART OF STONE

Feeling unwanted and unloved, Keely returns
to Jacobsville and to Boone Sinclair, a rancher
troubled by his own past. Boone has always
seemed reserved, but now Keely discovers a
sensuality with him that quickly turns to love. Can
they each see past their own scars to let love in?

*Available September 2008
wherever you buy books.*

SPECIAL EDITION™

Little did hotel-chain CFO Tom Holloway realize that his new executive assistant spelled trouble. But even though single mom Shelly Winston was planted by Holloway's worst enemy to take him down, Shelly was no dupe—she had a mind of her own and an eye for her handsome boss.

Look for

IN BED WITH THE BOSS

by *USA TODAY* bestselling author
CHRISTINE RIMMER

*Available July
wherever you buy books.*

#1 *NEW YORK TIMES* BESTSELLING AUTHOR
DEBBIE MACOMBER

What do you want most in the world?

Anne Marie Roche wants to find happiness again. At 38, she's childless, a recent widow and alone. On Valentine's Day, Anne Marie and several other widows get together to celebrate…what? Hope, possibility, the future. They each begin a list of twenty wishes.

Anne Marie's list includes learning to knit, doing good for someone else and falling in love again. She begins to act on her wishes, and when she volunteers at a school, little Ellen enters her life. It's a relationship that becomes far more important than she ever imagined, one in which they both learn that wishes can come true.

Twenty Wishes

"These involving stories…continue the Blossom Street themes of friendship and personal growth that readers find so moving."—*Booklist* on *Back on Blossom Street*

Available the first week of May 2008 wherever books are sold!

MIRA®

Harlequin American Romance is
celebrating its 25th anniversary
just in time to make your
Fourth of July celebrations
sensational with Kraft!

ALL-AMERICAN POTATO SALAD

Prep time:	Total:	Makes:
20 minutes	3 hours 20 minutes (incl. refrigerating)	8 servings, 1/2 cup each

1-1/3 lb new potatoes cubed (about 4 cups), cooked
12 slices OSCAR MAYER Center Cut bacon, cut into 1-inch
 pieces, cooked, drained
1/2 cup chopped green peppers
1/2 cup chopped onions
1/2 cup MIRACLE WHIP dressing
1/2 tsp salt
1/8 tsp black pepper

(Continued on next page)

ALL-AMERICAN POTATO SALAD *(continued)*

TOSS potatoes, bacon, green peppers and onions in large bowl.

ADD dressing, salt and black pepper; toss to coat. Cover.

REFRIGERATE several hours or until chilled.

Kraft Kitchens' Tips

Substitute:
Prepare as directed, using MIRACLE WHIP Light Dressing.

Serving Suggestion:
Serve this classic potato salad with grilled chicken breasts and a fresh fruit salad.

Jazz it Up:
Stir in 1 tbsp GREY POUPON Dijon mustard before chilling.

Each Harlequin American Romance book
in June contains a different recipe from
the world's favorite food brand, Kraft.
Collect all four to have a complete
Fourth of July meal right at your fingertips!

For more great meal ideas please visit
www.kraftfoods.com.

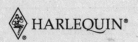 HARLEQUIN®

 *American ★ Romance*®

COMING NEXT MONTH

#1217 SMOKY MOUNTAIN REUNION by Lynnette Kent
The State of Parenthood
The last time Nola Shannon saw Mason Reed was at her high school graduation. Twelve years later she still carries a torch for the handsome teacher—now a widowed father. And Mason's certainly never forgotten *her*. He and his young son need someone special in their lives. Could the lovely, caring Nola be that someone?

#1218 HANNAH'S BABY by Cathy Gillen Thacker
Made in Texas
It's the happiest day of her life when Hannah brings her adopted baby home to Texas. But what would make the new mother *really* happy is a daddy to complete their instant family. And Hannah's friend Joe Daugherty would make a perfect father. He just doesn't know it yet!

#1219 THE FAKE FIANCÉE by Megan Kelly
What's a man to do when his mother wants him to have a family so badly she ambushes him with blind dates? Hire the caterer to be his fiancée, that's what. His mom is thrilled, but will Joe Riley and Lisa Meyer's pretend engagement become the real thing?

#1220 TRUST A COWBOY by Judy Christenberry
The Lazy L Ranch
When Pete Ledbetter's granddad decides to find Pete a wife, the bachelor cowboy has no choice but to get his own decoy bride-to-be. He looks no further than his family's Colorado dude ranch. After a summer romance, he knew he was compatible with chef Mary Jo Michaels. But after their summer breakup, he knew winning back her trust would be nearly impossible....

www.eHarlequin.com